An excerpt from
Molly's Lips: Club Mephisto Retold

Mephisto looked under the desk, at Molly's face pressed against her Master's shin. "She seems happy. Content."

"If she ever told you otherwise...this week, or anytime...I hope you would let me know."

"Of course I would."

"She might talk more openly to you than to me."

"Or less openly. She doesn't know me very well."

Clayton grimaced, just for a moment, a small show of emotion from the staunchly reserved man. "She doesn't know me very well either, to tell the truth. She knows her Master, and I know my slave. But truly, if I thought for a moment that wasn't what she wanted..."

"As I said, she seems very content. If I learn anything to the contrary this week, I'll let you know. My guess is she'll be running to your arms as soon as I'm done with her."

Clayton laughed, his spirits seeming to lift. "It would disappoint me very much if you didn't challenge her this week. She's become quite skilled at satisfying me and being my good girl. I only require her to look pretty, behave obediently, and service me sexually. But I believe you'll be another matter."

"I'll try to be another matter," Mephisto said with a grin.

Molly's Lips:

Club Mephisto Retold

By

Annabel Joseph

Other erotic romance by Annabel Joseph

Mercy
Cait and the Devil
Firebird
Deep in the Woods
Fortune
Owning Wednesday
Lily Mine
Comfort Object
Caressa's Knees
Odalisque
Cirque du Minuit
Burn For You

Erotica by Annabel Joseph

Club Mephisto

Coming soon:

The Edge of the Earth (as Molly Joseph)
Command Performance
Disciplining the Duchess

To Begin...

Hopefully you understand something at the outset: this story has been told before.

If you haven't read *Club Mephisto*, this will all be new to you. If you did read *Club Mephisto*, you'll know this story—but only from the submissive point of view. In that book, I clung to Molly's surrendered worldview from beginning to end so you, the reader, could gain insight into why she made the choices she did, and why she was so overjoyed to be returned to her Master's embrace.

But there was another story going on the whole time—Mephisto's story. The voice of Mephisto, Molly's mentor and temporary Master, was always alive in my mind as I wrote, an ongoing echo to Molly's thoughts. In the end I found I had to put his "echo" to paper, since his point of view comes with so many surprising revelations.

So yes, you may have read this story before, but I hope you'll find Mephisto's retelling wholly new and fascinating, and make a discovery similar to the one I've made—that Master and slave, dominant and submissive, giver and taker are essentially two sides of the same coin. I hope you will also want to read *Burn For You*, the novel length conclusion to the Molly and Mephisto saga. You'll find an excerpt from *Burn For You* at the end of this novella.

As always, I offer this caveat: This story and its companion, *Club Mephisto*, are not traditional romances. They depict total power exchange relationships which contain aspects of hardcore BDSM, sadomasochism, partner sharing, m/m/f and m/f/m threesomes, orgies, deep objectification, caging, extended chastity denial, anal play and intercourse, and other edgy forms of connection.

This book is not a romance.

Well, not to most people.

To my Molly and Mephisto lovers, thanks for understanding.

This book is for you.

Mephisto

In the beginning, when Mephisto first met Molly, he'd hoped she might be his. She'd flirted with him in a skittish kind of way, and he'd found her appealing. Pretty, dark haired, petite, and charmingly rough around the edges. Okay, she'd been a mess, but that had compelled him most of all.

Then Clayton Copeland showed up, and the whole matter had been lifted from his hands.

Mephisto didn't begrudge them their happiness. Every time he saw them together, he knew they were meant to be. Not in a romantic sense, because Mephisto wasn't much into romance. No, in a realistic sense. They simply made a perfect pair. Perfect Master, perfect slave.

Mephisto scrutinized the gentleman sitting across from him, his friend and occasional lunch companion. Late forties, with just a touch of gray in his blond hair. Filthy rich, cordial and debonair. Clayton's suit must have cost a cool five thousand, and his shoes... Mephisto didn't care to contemplate how much they'd set the man back. Not that Clayton Copeland would feel it in his very, *very* deep wallet.

If the wait staff in the glossy, contemporary eatery found them an odd lunch pair, they were too well trained to show it. Clayton was rich enough not to care what people thought of his friends, and Mephisto, as the owner of an exclusive fetish club, was not in the habit of apologizing for his piercings, dreadlocks, or gothic style of dress. Mephisto was also well off, though not as wealthy as his friend. Far from blond and blue eyed, Mephisto was dark, with eyes so deep brown they appeared to be black. Great for intimidating submissive women—and sometimes their dominants too.

Mephisto used his ability to frighten when it suited him. For instance, during scenes at his club when he acted as top, or to intervene in scenes that got out of hand. At other times, like now, in the company of an old friend, he let the tough-guy posturing fall away. He moved sushi around on his plate in a fit of OCD, perhaps induced by the spartan aesthetic of the Japanese bar. He waved a chopstick at Clayton.

"So, explain it again. Without the legalese."

Clayton chuckled. "The legalese is necessary. I want her to be provided for, and I want it to be ironclad."

Mephisto made a face. "Why wouldn't it be ironclad?"

"Because my family is a collection of heartless and mercenary jackasses. Molly couldn't stand up to them if they tried to challenge anything. And they would—unless it's ironclad. They've always considered her an interloper. My social-climbing trophy wife. If only they knew."

Mephisto popped some sushi in his mouth and considered the man across the table. There was a gravity to his expression

Mephisto didn't see too often. "You've got the best lawyers, Clay. I'm sure Molly will be fine."

The older man's lips tightened. "See, that's the thing. I don't think she'll be fine. Not emotionally, or any way else." He put down his chopsticks and leaned on the table. "I've stripped away every vestige of self-possession from that girl. Thoroughly and methodically."

"With her consent," Mephisto interjected quietly.

"Yes, of course, with her consent. But that will be small comfort to her if I die and leave her alone."

"Downer alert."

Clayton shrugged. "I want everything in order, just in case. I'm twenty years older than her. I'm starting to feel my age."

"You don't look it. Come on, you might live fifty more years."

"Perhaps." Clayton's lips twisted in a rueful smile. "If I do, I hope she lives fifty years and a day. If she dies before me—"

Mephisto made an impatient sound. "For real, this is maudlin. What the fuck is going on with you?"

Clayton shook his head and leaned back again in his chair. "Nothing. Just the fretting of an aging man who's made himself the center of a young woman's world." He steepled his fingers and looked up at the ceiling. "She's my slave, but she's also my wife. The love of my life. My happiness."

Mephisto felt a pang of something. Jealousy? He had plenty of slaves, plenty of submissive women and men who formed a constantly revolving constellation around him. But he didn't have anything like Molly's kind of love. Clayton gave him a direct, intent look.

"So, I'll get to the point of this conversation, and why I asked you here today. Jay, if I die, I want you to take care of her. I mean, watch out for her. You know what I mean."

It sobered Mephisto, to hear his real name on Clayton's lips. He didn't use it very often. His scene name had become his new name over the years. "Sure," he said at once. "Of course I'll look after her. You didn't even have to ask." Hell, Mephisto had been looking after her since he'd stumbled into her at a Pike Street nightclub. He was the one who'd guided her into Clayton's arms. Reluctantly, but still.

"I mean, the financial stuff, the legal stuff, all that will be taken care of," Clayton assured him. "She'll have plenty of money, enough to live her whole life in whatever way she wants."

"You just want me to be sure she finds that 'whatever way she wants' after you're gone."

"Exactly." Clayton looked relieved, his shoulders losing a little of their tension. "And I really want her to have whatever she wants. A new Master, if she wants it, as soon as she wants it."

Mephisto frowned. "Do you really think she'll want to go barreling right into another relationship like the one she had with you?"

"I'm absolutely sure of it," Clayton replied without a second's pause. "My fear is that she won't have the emotional and social strength to navigate herself into another safe harbor, so to speak."

"Especially if she's still mourning you."

"Yes."

"And she'll be rich then, right? A rich widow at large."

Clayton rubbed his eyes. "I can't stand to think about it."

"You don't have to think about it." Mephisto started rearranging sushi again as the waitress stopped by to refill their plates. She slid Mephisto a sultry look as she sashayed away. And, oh, he really had a thing for Asian girls. He forced his gaze back to Clayton. "Look, worry no more. When you go— If you go—I will be there for her one hundred percent."

"Even if I'm not gone...if I'm incapacitated somehow…"

Mephisto threw up his hands. "Now you're just annoying me."

"I'm serious. If I can no longer be the Master she needs, for whatever reason, help her. Help her accept it. Help her move on."

"She won't leave you, you know. No matter what. You could have five kinds of cancer, Alzheimer's, Lou Gehrig's disease and the Black Plague and she'd still be kneeling at your bedside in her submissive pose, waiting for instructions."

Clayton grimaced. "I know. At that point I'd like you to drag her away. Seduce her away if you have to."

At the mention of seduction, a chill fell over the table. If Clayton knew of Mephisto's original interest in Molly, he never revealed it. He'd simply accepted Mephisto's gift. And Molly had been a gift, given many years ago in selfless goodwill. Mephisto could have molded Molly into his own lover. She would have been exciting, challenging. She was a contradictory combination of reckless and submissive. Sometimes Mephisto wondered if he hadn't been a little afraid of taking her on. Clayton had been a better match, with his cool, implacable manner. Maybe Mephisto and Molly would have been too volatile a combination.

Clayton watched him. Yeah, maybe he knew. "You've taken good care of her," Mephisto said, just to say something. "It's very satisfying to me, to know I put her into such good hands. I hope you live a long, happy Black-Plague-free life with her, and that you both die together holding hands, lying under a rainbow in a field of flowers."

"That would be nice," Clayton said. "But unlikely."

"Does Molly know you've made all these arrangements for her?"

Clayton shook his head. "Not yet. It would alarm her. I'll bring it up sometime when the mood is right. She can be so emotional."

"Would it be easier if I talked to her about it? Let her know I'd be around if something happened to you?"

"I think that might scare her." Clayton paused, taking a sip of tea. "She's rather scared of you, you know."

"Maybe some time when work is blowing up, or you're heading out of town, you can leave her with me for a while. We could get more comfortable with each other." The words were out before Mephisto fully considered the repercussions. He looked up at Clayton and saw only enthusiasm.

"That's a great idea. She shouldn't be afraid of you. And in that situation you could get to know her better at the same time. Learn firsthand what makes her tick."

The privilege of the revered Master, to not feel one inkling of jealous suspicion. Mephisto took a breath and nodded. "I'd like that. I didn't get to know her very well before she became yours. She never submitted to me." Mephisto tried to ignore the sudden surge of lustful curiosity in his veins. What would it be like to be the recipient of such submission? It wouldn't be the submission she showed her true Master, but a fascinating opportunity all the same. "And you could set whatever parameters you wished," Mephisto added, trying not to sound too guilty. "Whatever would make you most comfortable."

Clayton waved a hand. "I would give you full use of her, of course, if you kept her. It would only confuse her to do otherwise. As long as the typical protocols are observed...condoms and such. Safe, sane, consensual."

"Of course."

Clayton laughed. "As if you would accept anything else. I know those are your club's protocols. And ah...I would really enjoy subjecting her to some of your more rigorous instructional training sessions. It would be good for her," he said with another chuckle. "You're a much stricter Master than I am. And you'd be less emotionally involved. I spoil her so badly sometimes."

Mephisto had to smile. Clayton might spoil her, but he had no compunction about throwing her under Mephisto's bus to get his jollies. "I would be sure to put her through her paces while you were away. Not that she isn't already well trained."

"You're a good friend," Clayton said. "You've always been such a generous friend to me. We'll set something up soon. A short sojourn at Club Mephisto—I'm sure Molly will be delighted."

Mephisto wasn't so sure, but that was part of the thrill.

Molly

It was just a few weeks after their conversation that Clayton called Mephisto about taking Molly. He had a last minute business trip, some real estate clients to meet in New York. Clayton called right from work, sounding harried and anxious, and was glad to hear Mephisto expected a quiet week.

Even if he hadn't, Mephisto would have cleared it for her.

The club was in full swing when Molly arrived with her Master. Slow, pulsing house music accompanied throaty moans and shrieks from the various play spaces. Mephisto watched as Clayton affixed a silver leash to her slim metal collar at the door. She was as lovely as ever. Pretty shiny dark curls and pale skin. Lovely kissable lips and a curvy, feminine body, even though she was small. She reminded Mephisto of a kitten. She crawled gracefully enough at her Master's side, but you got the feeling if you moved too fast, she'd leap behind him and cower, her eyes wide and frightened. He got a bit hard thinking about it—and this lovely kitten would be his for a whole week. Mephisto would take advantage, but not mindlessly. He would try to return Molly in better condition than he received her. It was his usual goal when tops handed over their bottoms for Mephisto's special brand of "training." But most of those training sessions were short. An hour. A day.

In this case he'd agreed to look after Molly for a week. What could he do to her in a week? What would he teach her? How could he broaden her submission and challenge her mind? Without, of course, royally fucking her up? That was the rub. Any extreme mindfucks were out of the question. Mild mindfucks? Oh yes.

Mephisto greeted Clayton first, before turning his attention to the woman at his feet. She glanced at him only briefly before she dropped her gaze. He tried to read her face, whether she felt excitement or nervousness, but her eyes were now fixed on her Master's shoes. Mephisto touched her head lightly, to welcome her, or perhaps soothe her. "Your lovely kitten," he said to Clayton. "She's looking as sleek and fine as ever."

Mephisto led Clayton across the carpeted common area, past the surrounding play spaces to the large table that served as his desk, tucked away at the back of the club. He was charmed by the way Molly curled up at her Master's feet as soon as he sat. He wondered if she would make a fuss when Clayton left. Or *after* he left. Mephisto could always quiet her down in the cage.

Mephisto exchanged niceties with Clayton while he gestured to the bar for refreshments. He watched absently as Ginger fixed their drinks, remembering Molly working behind that bar, oh, years ago now. There was almost no way to reconcile the Molly he'd first met with the woman now resting under his desk. He'd met Molly when she was just out of college, sharp as a tack, and harboring a death wish. Not overtly. She'd never said to him, "I want to die," but her actions proved otherwise. Drugs, partying,

15

cozying up to all the wrong people who did all the wrong things to her. She'd lost her environmental job with City Parks and soon after lost her apartment. She hopped from bed to bed, sometimes partying around the clock for days. Once they became better friends, she was in and out of Club Mephisto, either manic or falling apart. Mephisto watched until he couldn't watch anymore, and then he strong-armed her into working for him, just so he'd know where she spent her nights.

She'd been like a hollow shell then. Full of hate, wanting to please and yet despising herself. Mephisto had been at a loss, not sure how to handle her, but then Clayton had stepped up and put an end to all her nonsense for good. Somehow, within weeks, he'd turned Molly from a seething, neurotic monster to a contented slave. Mephisto wasn't sure about the morality of it all; he just knew she had to be happier now. Didn't she?

Across the club, a woman cried out at the height of a flogging scene, a cry of agony and joy. Mephisto's whole life was power exchange, the thrill and emotion of the lifestyle, the cavernous dark club that served as his home, but even he was left puzzled sometimes by the people who moved in his world. Molly was still a puzzle to him.

What if she's not happy?

Molly stayed so rigidly in role. Clayton was holding her face now, giving her water from a cup. So helpless, so dependent. It was sexy, sure. But all the time?

"Do you ever give her breaks?" The question was out, random and abrupt, before Mephisto could stop it.

"Breaks?" asked Clayton.

"Breaks. When she's just your wife and not your slave?"

Clayton thought a moment. "You have to understand that, for us, they're the same things. It's just...me and Molly. This is how we are."

"Of course. But she never rebels? Fights the dynamic?"

"Surprisingly, no. I know you told me she used to be very rebellious."

"She was a hair-raising nightmare of a hellion, my friend."

Clayton laughed. "Well, she's not now. And no, she rarely rebels. Disobeys, perhaps, due to her own weakness or mistakes. But she takes her punishment and we move on." The older man shifted and lowered his voice. "I would let her take breaks if she wanted it. If she needed it. Sometimes I wish..." He stopped, rubbing his chin. "There are times I wish I saw more of her than the slave."

"Does she know you feel that way?"

"We've talked about it." Clayton shrugged. "You know, we've been married for many years. We've had conversations of excruciating closeness and honesty, and she tells me this is what she wants. No breaks. No moments of equality."

Mephisto looked under the desk, at Molly's face pressed against her Master's shin. "She seems happy. Content."

"If she ever told you otherwise...this week, or anytime...I hope you would let me know."

"Of course I would."

"She might talk more openly to you than to me."

"Or less openly. She doesn't know me very well."

Clayton grimaced, just for a moment, a small show of emotion from the staunchly reserved man. "She doesn't know me very well either, to tell the truth. She knows her Master, and I know my slave. But truly, if I thought for a moment that wasn't what she wanted..."

"As I said, she seems very content. If I learn anything to the contrary this week, I'll let you know. My guess is she'll be running to your arms as soon as I'm done with her."

Clayton laughed, his spirits seeming to lift. "It would disappoint me very much if you didn't challenge her this week. She's become quite skilled at satisfying me and being my good girl. I only require her to look pretty, behave obediently, and service me sexually. But I believe you'll be another matter."

"I'll try to be another matter," Mephisto said with a grin.

"Feel free to handle her as you wish, within the limits we talked about. I just wanted to give you a sense of what she's accustomed to."

"Certainly. That helps me. And just to reiterate, these are the limits we've outlined here." Mephisto handed over a temporary contract he'd written up for the length of Molly's stay. "No scarring or body modification, no unprotected sex. What about withholding of food and water?"

"I'll leave that to you." Clayton shrugged. "I know I can trust you to act responsibly." He reached under the table to pet his slave while they went over a few more medical emergency and legal release issues.

"Don't worry, Clayton. I won't break your toy," Mephisto finally assured him. "I plan to keep her in my rooms most of the time, and even when I bring her out to share, she'll be well-protected. As you know, my private parties are even more exclusive than my club events. I am very careful about who I allow to use my slaves. Now, if you don't mind, may I address your slave for a moment? On her feet?"

"Certainly." Clayton tugged Molly's leash. She stood up beside her Master, looking slightly dazed.

Clayton slid a hand down her arm, smiling at her. "Master Mephisto wishes to speak to you, Molly. Stand up straight now, girl. No cringing."

Mephisto half expected her to burst into tears. Clayton's little silver leash dangled between her breasts, moving slightly at each deep breath. Mephisto tilted her chin up, forcing her to look at him.

"Molly, I promised your Master to take good care of you this week with his permission, but I require consent from one more person."

"Yes, Sir," she said in a quiet but surprisingly level voice.

"Do you agree to act as my slave this week, giving me your complete trust and obedience?"

"Yes, Sir. If it pleases my Master."

Mephisto smiled at the man to his right. Clayton scolded her in an impatient tone. "Answer for yourself, Molly. Do you consent? Leave me out of it for the moment. He requires your permission."

"But Master! I don't want to leave you out of it."

"Enough," Mephisto said, laughing. "That works for me, Clayton. I'm getting the sense that as long as you're willing, she's willing." He sobered and looked back at her. "What a very smitten slave you are. Your Master is fortunate."

Clayton shot him a look, and it struck Mephisto for the first time what a burden a relationship like that would be. This parting was certainly difficult—for both of them. For Clayton, to give up control, and for Molly to lose his control. Mephisto had many slaves he played with, but none of them were a full time responsibility like Molly was to Clayton. For just a moment, Mephisto's confidence faltered. Could he do this? Could he deliver her back to Clayton without turning her into a total wreck?

"I suppose I'd better go," said Clayton. "She's cutting off the circulation in my legs."

Under the table, her face was again pressed to her Master's pant leg. Mephisto wanted to find it silly, but it was touching. "I'll take good care of her," he promised.

"Well then, she's yours," Clayton said, handing over her leash.

Mephisto watched Molly for signs of distress. Her eyes were wet, her expression bleak, but she was hanging in there. He tugged the leash to bring her up on her knees. "Bid your Master goodbye, kitten. You'll see him in a week."

Clayton leaned down to give her one last squeeze. Their hug looked natural, like they did it a lot. She clung to him, her face buried against the side of his neck.

"Now, no tears," her Master said. He whispered something against her ear that Mephisto couldn't hear while he ran a hand down her back and over her ass. Mephisto started to think he might have to unlock one of the back rooms for an impromptu goodbye fuck, but Clay finally pulled away from her. He rose and left, not looking back. Molly knelt like a statue, staring after him. All around them, erotic, theatrical BDSM scenes continued, but Mephisto was riveted by the simple drama of Molly's tense shoulders and back. She tracked Clayton until he exited the club and then still she watched the door, like he might somehow materialize there again. Change his mind and return for her.

Poor slave.

Mephisto gave her leash a tug. "Eyes on me."

She dragged her gaze to his. He made his eyes intentionally hard, so the moisture beneath her lids didn't dissolve into rivers of tears. She looked beautifully fearful and miserable, trying so hard not to break down.

"I don't think you'll be worth much tonight," he said. "We'll begin tomorrow, after you rest. But first..."

He drew her forward, encountering no resistance, and had her kneel under the desk between his legs. Beneath her nervousness and sadness, he saw something else that pleased him. Curiosity. He was feeling it too. He'd been her boss many years ago, but never her lover. Never her Master. He unzipped, half-hard from anticipation. Her touch was hesitant at first, exploratory. She kissed and fondled him, and he relaxed, enjoying her skilled caresses. He handed down a flavored condom and then leaned back, spreading his legs slightly. She fumbled around with the rubber until he gave her leash a little yank of impatience. She'd have to get quicker with that.

When the condom was finally on, she went right to work. No one could see her, but they could probably tell from his face what was going on under the desk. He didn't care. Oh, God, he didn't give a flying fuck once she got going. Molly was every bit as talented as he'd expected her to be. She licked from the base of his cock to the head and back again, not letting the condom impede her. Her mouth was warm and slippery, and she kept a nice grip on his balls, not too loose and listless but not too tight.

"Holy Christ," he said under his breath as one of the dungeon monitors came up to his desk. "What is it?"

"Is everything okay?" Jared asked.

"Everything's fine," he drawled back. "What do you need?"

"Madam Moxy wants to know if she can use the back stage at midnight tomorrow."

Madam Moxy's scenes tended to get out of hand, but she was a popular figure in the community. Mephisto looked at Jared. "Are you working?" He nodded. "Ask Sam if he can come in. The two of you can put down any shit that gets stirred up." *Oh my God, she sucks cock like an angel.* He bit back a groan and eyed Jared. "Anything else?"

"No, sir," Jared said, finally seeming to notice that Mephisto's attention was otherwise occupied. Mephisto sighed and reached down to grip the back of Molly's neck and ease his cock a little deeper in her throat. No flinch, no resistance. After a long, thrilling stroke he let her take a breath and then invaded her mouth again, basking in the warmth and tightness of her lips.

He looked around the club absently, letting her serve him, letting the pleasure pulse and grow at the base of his pelvis in time to the music in the background. A few other patrons walked by, greeting him with knowing smiles. After ten minutes or so, it was too hard to focus on anything but the pleasure he felt. He closed his eyes and rested his head against the back of the chair, enjoying every delicate kiss, every bold stroke of her tongue. He was gripping her leash now, his hand opening and closing on the table.

Perhaps in some response to the tension in his body, she sucked faster, pumping the lower part of his cock, building a crest of sensation. She sucked and licked the head, then flicked his balls with the tip of her tongue. He felt a trembling and pulsing begin, the onset of orgasm. With a gasp he held her head and thrust deep. After the drawn-out, expert blowjob, every one of his nerves responded. Firecracker climax. His whole body contorted as his cock emptied out in a bone-trembling release. He dropped his head on the desk, his hand still cupping the back of her neck.

Through some haze of thought, or maybe her sudden trembling, he realized she couldn't breathe. He let her draw away, and ordered her to be still while he turned and stood on jelly legs to take off the condom and refasten his jeans. The dungeon was getting busier, and he was suddenly feeling a need for control. He beckoned one of his slaves, Lila, to come and assist him before he gave the leash in his hand a tug. He would put Molly away for the night and get his head in the right place to begin mastering her tomorrow. He led her back through heavy double doors into his private residence, past the living room and kitchen and into his bedroom.

When they entered his room, he saw her eye the large, low cage comprising the underside of his bed, and the larger cage in the corner. She would need to be caged tonight. It would help her feel secure and enslaved—even though she wasn't his slave. At a signal, Lila started to arrange blankets and pillows in the corner enclosure. Lila had slept there a time or two herself, although she had her own place and was only a part-time playmate for Mephisto. For Lila, the cage was a treat. Sometimes, over the next week, the cage would feel like a treat for Molly too.

He pulled his charge to her feet and forced her eyes up to his.

"You are no doubt tired," he said. "Rest tonight, because tomorrow you will serve me at my leisure, and probably need to learn a lot of new things."

She nodded, her eyes wide. "Yes, Master. I'll try my best to serve you."

"Yes, you will—or I'll demand you try again and again until you get it right. Perfectly right. And for the duration of your stay here, kitten," he continued, "you will abide by the same rules your Master set regarding touching yourself."

"Yes, Master." She shifted a little, looking more tired than turned on, but with slave types, you never knew what cages might inspire them to do.

He gave her a dire look. "You will not want to discover what happens if you disobey me in this, girl. Understand?"

"Yes, Master," she said, nodding. "I understand."

"Now Lila will show you to the bathroom, where you will shower, wash your hair, and brush your teeth with the toiletries set aside for you on the counter. You will leave things clean and orderly when you're finished, and then Lila will put you to bed."

He nodded to the cage, needlessly. She understood. He thought for a moment of checking in with her. *Do you miss your Master? Is everything okay with you?* But such softness would have made both of them uncomfortable at this time when his authority had to be most strictly applied. So instead, he gave a last short nod to Lila and left the room. He had business to do, a club to monitor. Other slaves to torment and fuck. The night was young.

But Molly's night was over. He kept an eye on the monitor near his desk for the next half hour or so to be sure she settled down. She pushed on the door of the cage a few times, tried the padlock, but she wasn't trying to get out. She was checking. *Yes, you're really locked in. You're not going anywhere until I let you.*

She laid back, her body still. No, not completely still. She moved her hands, ran them over the welts on her ass. He watched, ready to rush in and raise hell if she slid them between her thighs, but she didn't. She was crying. Did the welts still hurt? They weren't that fresh. Clayton had probably done them earlier in the evening. Mephisto finally realized that she was crying over Clayton, caressing the marks he'd left on her.

These wretches in love. He took a screen shot and emailed it to Clayton with the subject "Lucky Bastard" and the simple text, "All is fine." Shortly after, she turned away, but her shoulders still shook. He wanted to see those tears, demand them for himself. He wanted to taste them, but the club was busy and he had other things to do. He left her to her dreams of Clayton and lost himself instead in the fervor of Club Mephisto on a Friday night.

The First Day

Mephisto woke earlier than usual. He wasn't sure why, but then she shifted in her cage and he heard her. "*Please. Please...*"

Her voice sounded thick, anxious. It held a note of panic that made him hot. He shifted and turned on his bedside light so he could see her. She was still asleep. "*No... Please...*"

What did slaves dream about? He couldn't imagine. Mephisto had begun his journey as an s-type but found it didn't suit him. It wasn't enough for him to serve and receive. It didn't offer enough creative opportunity for his tastes. He still bottomed now and again when he was in the mood to really disintegrate.

There weren't many people strong enough to top him when he got that way.

Mephisto got up to take a piss, shower and shave, then laid back down and drowsed to her occasional noises of distress. He couldn't tell if she was upset or turned on when she was repeating *please, please...* Masochists. Who ever understood them?

Eventually she shifted, turned over and reached out, whacking her hands on the bars. Ouch.

That jogged her awake and her eyes flew open. He watched her come to complete consciousness, remembering where she was and what she was doing in a cage. She stared at him. He was lying on top of the covers, buck naked and mostly hard. He couldn't help but be flattered by the way she stared. He stroked himself just to see her eyes widen even more. Jesus, she played the innocent act like a virtuosa. Trouble was, he knew her way back when...

She smiled then, a small, impish smile that took him by surprise.

"Do I amuse you?" he asked.

Alarm replaced mirth. "No...no, Master. I was only thinking...well."

"Only thinking what?"

"I was wondering why you don't walk around the club naked when your physique is so...worthy of admiration, Master."

Mephisto leveled her with his best Casanova look. "Are you admiring me?"

She averted her eyes. "Master, if only you had awakened me, I might have served you rather than making you wait."

"I wake you when I like, and you serve me when I say so."

"I'm sorry, Master."

"You were talking in your sleep."

"I'm sorr—"

"Stop apologizing. I'm just telling you. I didn't wake you because I was watching you talk in your sleep. It was rather fascinating, actually." He shifted and stretched, wondering what he would do with his lovely borrowed slave today. Besides humiliate her by making her ask to go to the bathroom.

"Did you sleep well last night?" he asked with a sigh, scratching his stomach.

"Yes, Master." Shifting. Pressing her legs together.

"You cried a little when Lila put you in there," he said, raising one brow.

"I did cry a little. I missed my Master."

"I'm your Master for now. Or were you crying for me?"

She shifted again, eying the bars and the padlock that held her trapped. She looked back at him with a charming little blush.

"Master...um...I need to use the restroom. Please."

"You will, when I tell you to."

She lifted her chin a little, a very subtle sign of annoyance he caught all the same. He stroked his cock again, enjoying her discomfort for a few more moments before he crossed to unlock her cage. It wouldn't be very nice to send her back to Clayton with a UTI. "Go on, then. Quickly," he said, reaching down to help her out of the enclosure. "Take care of things."

She scurried off to the bathroom, leaving the door open. He stood and waited beside her cage, listening to endless peeing and then sounds of her making herself presentable in a frenzied, hurried way. How terrified she must be. It was good, but bad. A certain level of anxiety would improve her submission. Too much anxiety would freeze her, even damage her. She appeared back at the door, taking him in with her deep blue eyes. Pretty eyes. She was so beautiful. Too beautiful.

"Come here."

Like most slaves, she moved with a great deal of self-awareness. She was tense and yet graceful, her smooth walk showing off all her feminine attributes—her little waist, her round hips, her trim shoulders and perfect breasts. When she was close enough, he took her in his arms, wanting to feel her against him.

27

His cock was rising again with a vengeance, sliding against her warm, smooth skin. He held her with one arm, using the other to cup her breasts. They were real, not too large and not too small, just round and firm and luscious in a feminine way. He ran his fingers over the pert globes gently at first, then pinched the nipples and squeezed them. He slapped them lightly to see how she'd react. She flinched a little, but didn't pull away. With a sigh of admiration, he tipped her face up to his.

"I've always found you the most enticing thing, kitten. So beautifully formed. Like a pretty vase." He stared down at her, tightening his grip around her waist. "But vases are breakable."

She drew in a halting breath and bit her lip. He searched her face, so familiar and yet so novel to him. So many expressions flitted across her features, one foremost—

"You're afraid," he said.

She blinked, and nodded slowly. "Yes, Master."

"Tell me why."

Molly was silent a moment, thinking. "You're a very strong man," she finally said. "I know to obey you, and I'll try, but there is nothing to protect me from you if...if you were moved to anger."

So she thought him dangerous. It was a reputation he was guilty of promoting, however untrue it might be. "Your Master's directives protect you, to a degree. I will not hurt you beyond the limits I promised him last night. And believe me, I am a man of my word. But will you move me to anger?" He traced her smooth cheekbones, her lovely lips. "I suppose you might. I know your Master has trained you just as he wishes you. I know you are a well-trained little slave. But remember something, kitten. I am not your usual Master. You will need to learn and abide by my rules this week."

"Yes, Master." She huddled close to him even in her fear. He rubbed his cock across her belly and squeezed her welted ass, enjoying her little gasp of pain. Then he slapped her ass sharply.

"Nice marks. Punishment, or Master's pleasure?"

She thought a moment. "Both, I think."

He chuckled as he nudged her away. "Not so perfect after all." He slid a look over her body. His cock was about to burst, and she was a trembling little package of available flesh. "All right, kitten. I'm going to get to know you a little better. Go kneel on the bed. All fours. Open and hungry, like a bitch in heat."

She turned without a word to obey, crawling onto his white sheets. He stopped her near the edge, positioning her and then rolling on a condom. Her legs were spread and parted, her back arched as if she strained to accept him. Spectacular. He squeezed her welts one more time and then fastened his hands on her hips, driving into her roughly. The delicious sensation of tightness and warmth spurred on the ache that had been building ever since he'd opened his eyes.

He fucked her hard, mechanically, purposely seeking his own pleasure with no thought to hers. It was a quick and enjoyable way to put a slave into the right mind space. The rougher he was with her, the wetter she got.

"You like this?" he whispered. "Being fucked like a toy? You do, don't you?"

"Yes—Yes, Master." Her hips arched back as if to seek more of his selfish treatment. He gripped her hips tighter, lengthening his strokes.

"I'm just getting a feel for you," he said. "And letting you feel me. You're going to feel a lot of me this week." He guessed that was probably an unnecessary warning. Well, she was used to being used. He ran a hand up her spine, grabbing a handful of her hair. "You're nice and tight, aren't you, girl?"

"Yes, Master." She squirmed as his grip increased. "I—I try to stay tight for Master's pleasure."

"Good girl. Speaking of tight..."

Mephisto pulled out and pressed the head of his cock against her asshole. To his surprise, she tensed up, impeding him.

"Your Master told me you are anally trained," he said with a touch of impatience.

"I...I am, Master."

"You still need lubricant?"

"He uses a little. From my pussy."

The lube on the condom should have been perfectly sufficient for a slave of her training, but then she was nervous. He went for lube and shoved a generous amount into her tight hole. She still resisted, but this time the lube eased his way whether she wanted his thick tool in her ass or not. She groaned as the head stretched her, and then seemed to resign herself as the rest of his length slid in. He waited a moment, just enjoying the sheer, animal pleasure of forcing her. Her ass gripped him, heady sexual friction adding flames to the fire. Again, he took up a jerky, mechanical rhythm that drove sparks of heat down his cock to his ass and balls.

"Mm. Very tight," he said, gripping her shoulders to make her feel trapped, used. He wondered if she was enjoying herself. Her pained groan during his penetration had been replaced by subtle little sighs of lust. As a warning, he reached beneath her and wrenched both her nipples.

"Oh, Master... Please..."

Please, please... Just like in her dreams. She pulled away from him but he only held her tighter, his cock buried to the hilt.

"Don't come," he warned. "A little reminder. If I don't tell you to come, don't dare."

Mephisto enjoyed making women come, he really did. He enjoyed female sexuality, delighted in the way women fell apart in the throes of climax. But at the moment, he enjoyed controlling and dominating Molly more. Denying her orgasms would help establish his mastery over her, and also make her frustrated and horny. Both results served his purposes well. He increased the rhythm of his thrusts, pounding his hips against her. He came in a glorious wave, all the tension of the morning dissolving, spurted out into his slave's tight anal channel. He pulled away slowly, commanding Molly to stay as she was. He threw out the condom in the bathroom, washed up, and got a stainless steel plug from a cabinet in his room—a large one. She would soon understand he was big on anal accessibility.

"Can't let all that lube I had to use go to waste," he said, crossing back to stand behind her. He pressed the silver toy against her hole. It gave a little easier this time, but she still tensed and whimpered until he had the plug firmly seated inside her. "If we need to lube you up just to take my cock, you could probably benefit from some more training." Her head was bowed, her legs trembling, perhaps from enduring the invasion in her backside. "The correct answer is, 'Yes, Master, thank you for training my asshole.'"

"Yes, Master. Thank you for training my asshole," Molly repeated.

"Okay," he said, pulling her up off the bed. "Time for breakfast. I'm starved."

* * * * *

31

Mephisto took her to the kitchen and sat her on the floor beside his chair while he cooked breakfast. Simple stuff, but he liked a hot breakfast. Egg white omelets, pancakes, toast. She sat in silence and watched him. Perhaps she felt a little ashamed at her nakedness. Or her uselessness. Clayton had told him she couldn't cook, couldn't even boil water. If she was his slave, Mephisto would have taught her to make the things he liked most, but she wasn't his slave and she was only going to be with him a week.

Once he finished cooking, he sat and ate, occasionally handing down tidbits from his fingers and sips of juice. She waited patiently. No begging eyes, which was kind of unfortunate because that would have entertained him. Afterward, feeling slightly piqued, he set her to washing all the dishes and pans by hand. She didn't even have a clue how to do that correctly, but she tried. Useless for anything but sex.

"Not much of a housekeeper, are you?" he asked.

The dish she was holding fell into the sink with a clatter. "I'm sorry, Master."

"What do you actually do for him?"

She turned to him, her face held carefully blank. "My Master keeps a housekeeper and chef for tasks like these. I am mainly to serve as...to serve for—"

"For his pleasure. Pleasure slave," Mephisto provided. "You have the looks to pull it off. I suppose he doesn't like you ruining those expensive French manicures he pays for."

She looked down at her nails, then started back to the dishes. "Yes, Master."

"What do you do all day? He sends you out shopping?"

"I...I am mostly unclothed in his service. But he buys me some things according to his pleasure. For when we go out."

"How often does he take you out?"

32

"When it pleases him."

Mephisto rolled his eyes. "*'For his pleasure.' 'When it pleases him.'* You know the lines well. Now answer my question. How often does he take you out?"

Molly paused to think, carefully drying a plate and placing it on the counter. "At certain times, like at the holidays, we attend more parties and events than other times. But I would say on average he takes me out three to four times a month. Perhaps four or five times a year, I help entertain guests in our home."

"Vanilla guests?"

"Yes, Master. Work parties and dinners."

"I bet you're amazing at that sort of thing. Hostessing."

"I try to pleas—"

"Please your Master. Yes. Thanks for the recap. Besides pleasing him, what do you do with your time?"

Come on, Molly. Tell me something real. Something about you, not Master's pleasure. "I... Well, I read," she finally said.

Thank God. "What do you read?"

"Erotica. Current events. History books." She shrugged. "Whatever Master feels will improve me."

"Do you watch television? Go online?"

"No. Not without his supervision."

"What else do you do, besides read?"

"I exercise. Master has a gym and a pool. Sometimes I help Mrs. Jernigan with housework. But I'm not allowed in the kitchen."

"Why not?"

"I don't know. My Master's rules. He controls what I eat."

Interesting. And deviant. "Controlling can be fun. And you enjoy this control?" he asked.

"Oh, yes, Master. I'm so thankful for it."

"What if he grows tired of all the work of controlling you?"

He didn't say it cruelly, but he meant to be cruel. To throw her off balance. "You'll grow old, kitten," he continued in a low, prodding voice. "You won't be attractive to him forever, even if he does manage not to grow bored of you. What will you do then?"

She took a soft breath and let it out slowly. "I don't know, Master."

"Do you speak to your family?"

"Sometimes. Birthday and holidays. He doesn't keep me from them, but...we're not very close."

"Hmm." Mephisto didn't say anything else, only gestured for her to finish up. She ducked her head, seemingly relieved not to be questioned any more. She washed the silverware at the pace of a turtle and unwittingly scratched the bejeezus out of his favorite non-stick pan. Housekeeper from hell. She wiped down the counters and then spent a good minute and a half hanging the dishtowel just so over the bar beside the sink. Her drive to please, her meekness disturbed him almost as much as it endeared her to him. He crossed the kitchen, stood behind her and brushed a hand across the small of her back.

"Hold the bar," he said against her ear. "The one you just hung the towel over." She hesitated a moment, but obeyed. "Don't let go."

He left her there, stalked out of the kitchen to regain his composure. Knowing that she didn't play—not like his slaves—it confounded him. She really lived for her Master. She lived under his constant control and even now, when her Master was miles away, she was still his slave. Somehow, that stirred up all kinds of uncomfortable feelings in him.

He sorted through his implements and selected a small black whip. He stalked back to the kitchen. Clayton's welts were fading. He was going to put his own marks on her.

"Eyes forward," he ordered, putting a hand on her back to brace her. "Don't let go of the bar."

He slashed the whip across her ass cheeks. She jumped but he held her still, delivering a second blow. "Oh, Master. Please!" she begged.

He ignored her, giving her two more strokes in quick succession. She shimmied and went up on her toes, but he had to give it to her—she didn't let go of the bar. He pressed his palm harder on her back, held her down and striped the back of her ass and thighs until her panicked cries and squirming turned to resigned tears. Even then he kept going, breaking her down. "Please! Please..." she sobbed. In answer he whipped her right across the middle of her cheeks, over the base of the toy protruding from her ass.

He was as breathless as she was. He inspected the marks. No blood, but bright red welts that would certainly deepen to purple. She was calming, her sobs turning to sniffles.

"Hand me that wooden spoon, kitten."

At his quiet command, she tensed and looked up at the canister of tools on the counter, and burst into a fresh round of tears. She reached for the broad wooden spoon and handed it back to him. At his nudge, she took a shuddering breath and put her hands back on the bar. Poor hurting slave. He'd do some allover reddening, some shock and awe to give her something to think about at the start of their week. He smacked her hard and fast over the criss-cross of welts from the whip. She groaned and then a scream broke loose, of fear or desperation. He stopped, not because she screamed, but because he was finished. He'd gotten her to that *place*.

He put the wooden spoon down and watched her cry for a moment, lying limp against the counter she'd so painstakingly tidied up. She still held the bar in a death grip. He put his hands over hers, forced her fingers to open and let go. He lifted her with a hand under her arm, finding her face wet with tears. When she reached to wipe them away he stopped her and impulsively pressed his face to hers. What was it about tears? Especially tears caused by himself? She reached out, seeking comfort. He held her, his face still pressed to her cheek.

"I know that hurt you." She shook against him, not answering. He reached down to caress her scarlet ass cheeks. "I imagine your Master keeps your skin well-marked when you're at home."

"Ye—yes, Master," she stammered through tears.

"Like him, I can't resist marking that lovely ass of yours. Or at least refreshing the marks he left on you. For my pleasure," he added. "I wasn't punishing you for anything, you know."

Again, a little shudder. "Thank...Thank you for explaining that, Master."

"You're most welcome. Although, of course, you are never owed an explanation."

She was finally calming. He pulled away from her, running his hands down her arms.

"And I have enjoyed talking with you, and getting to know you a little better this morning. Although I warn you, very soon you'll be put on speech restriction. So don't get too used to these chats."

She looked surprised at that. He knew this was all new to her, and not Clayton's style. He took her face in his hands and gazed down at her. "Don't worry. You'll be okay. Speech restriction is just one more tool to help you give yourself up to me. One more layer of yourself to submit."

"Yes, Master," she murmured against his palm. She looked up at him then with a look of such vulnerability, such brave dread, that he had to kiss her, just once. His lips touched hers...so soft, so open. She made a little gasp, nearly inaudible, but it set off something inside him. He pulled her hard against him, wrapped her up so she couldn't get away, and then he really kissed her. He thrust his tongue between her lips and searched her mouth like he could find the answers there. *Why are you like this? What's going on inside you?* She responded at first, but then she stiffened and he let her go. She touched her lips, her gaze fixed somewhere in the center of his chest.

"Master, you honor me," she said softly in the silence.

What the fuck did that mean? Why the fuck had he kissed her like that? What the holy fuck was going on? He rubbed the back of his neck and then his crotch, his cock straining against the front of his jeans. "You arouse me," he said, like it was enough of an explanation. Maybe it was. A light touch on her shoulder had her falling to her knees. She sat and waited as he rolled on a condom, and then opened as he placed a firm hand on the back of her neck.

Oh, Molly. He didn't know if he said it out loud, or only thought it. When her lips were around his cock, it was hard to figure out anything at all.

* * * * *

He put her to work for the rest of the day cleaning and prepping Club Mephisto for the weekend crowd. Yes, Molly wasn't much of a housekeeper, but she did the tasks he gave her to the best of her ability, and with no whining at all. Around five he

37

fed her again, and then attached her by her leash to the leg of his desk as Club Mephisto's staff started showing up. Bulky bouncers and chatty bartenders, stone-faced dungeon monitors and professional D/s players he hired to keep the club's scenes rolling when the paying customers were laying low. Many of them threw glances at Molly; she used to work there, after all.

Finally he took her leash and made her crawl around with him while he did last minute rounds. Surely she was glad now that she'd paid such good attention to cleaning the floor. She was tired, starting to drag. He let one of the bouncers use her ass, just because she'd been prepped so nicely by the ass plug and Mephisto was too busy to fuck her himself. Josh knelt behind her on the floor and fucked her in front of everyone. She seemed too exhausted to be humiliated. She was pliant, sub-spacey. Done for the day.

Mephisto led her back to his room and unleashed her, nudging her toward the shower. Dirty, used, sleepy slave. She'd be happy for her cage tonight. He hoped she slept well—all in all, she'd been a very good girl and she deserved it. He sent a short text to Clayton. "Molly's fine. Sore ass, worn out. She misses you."

He left out the part about kissing her. Twice. She was his to use anyway, Clayton had said so. Mephisto played with several girls that night, but he didn't kiss any of them. He rarely kissed anyone. It was just her lips, he told himself. They were spectacular.

Oh hell. Tomorrow they'd have to play some new games.

The Second Day

The next morning was very much like the first. Routines. They were good for slaves. He fucked her pussy and her ass—and this time he didn't have to use nearly as much force to take her tight hole. She didn't want to endure another day of being plugged, undoubtedly. Quick learner. But he was moving on to other training today.

After breakfast he went out, leaving her under the supervision of the club's many cameras. He made it clear she wasn't to go anywhere at any time where she couldn't be seen. He pointed out the few areas that weren't monitored. The dark corners, the bathrooms and some of his back rooms. She wasn't to go into any of those. She didn't seem overly aroused this morning, which rather disturbed him, and cleaning the club was unlikely to make her more aroused. Still...he wouldn't take a chance on her stealing any forbidden orgasms. Not with the plans he had laid out for her.

Mephisto rode through downtown streets to his favorite fetish store. He hadn't put a slave into deep chastity for a long time, and he wasn't sure why he wanted it so much for Molly now. Perhaps because she'd once been so reckless. Perhaps to see if she was still reckless now, and only hiding her impulses really, really well. He sent a text to Clayton, only to have him call back a moment later.

"Why exactly do you need my slave's measurements?"

Mephisto laughed. "Let's just say I want to buy a surprise for her."

"You're evil," Clayton said. "Are you buying her a harness? Or lingerie?"

"A chastity belt. Now, do you know her measurements or not?"

As Mephisto suspected, her Master knew them to the half inch. He jotted down Clayton's numbers for her waist and hip measurements. A little more small talk, and then conversation turned back to his slave.

"Is she behaving? You're not putting her into chastity out of necessity?"

"No. Actually, she's been an angel so far. It's tough on her though. She's in this haze of mourning, to be honest. God, Clay," he added, laughing. "Don't die, okay? Ever."

"I'm trying not to. But as far as I know they haven't discovered the secret to immortality yet."

"Well, I'm going to try to distract her a little more today."

"With chastity?"

"It can have a way of filling up a horny slave's mind. We'll see."

"Is she that bad? Do I need to come back?"

"God, no. She'll be fine. She's a tough girl."

"Will you keep her in chastity until I return?" asked Clayton with enthusiasm. "That would be great. I mean, you could take your orgasms, of course."

"I don't know. If I'm going to do all the work of keeping her in chastity, I think I might want to enjoy the final result. Nothing like an orgasm-deprived slave letting loose on one's cock."

"True. Selfish ass."

Mephisto laughed. "Just like you, my friend."

Using Clayton's measurements, Mephisto bought a chastity harness in black leather. It was high quality, supple, soft, with notches to adjust the fit precisely and attachment points for plugs or dildos. The front was a convex metal plate, designed to prevent any contact for her clitoris when it started aching. It was wonderfully evil. His friend Lorna, the owner of the eponymously named shop, smirked in collusion with him as she wrapped it up.

"I sell a lot of chastity gear for men, but not so many for women," she said.

"That's because it's so fun to make women come. But sometimes—if you're in a patient enough mood—it's fun to not let them come."

Lorna gave him a look. "You're not a man known for your patience, Master Mephisto." She would know. She was one of the women who occasionally managed to top him, with great effort on her part.

He winked at her. "We'll have to get together soon, Mistress. Perhaps when this slave I'm looking after has me nice and worn down."

Lorna's eyes flashed. "I don't want you worn down. That makes it so much less fun."

"When do I get to wear you down?" he asked seductively.

Lorna made a sound between a laugh and a snort. "Whoever you're looking after, she's scrambled your brains. Get out of here. Go back to your unfortunate subbie and strap her into that thing. Return when you're ready to kneel at my feet, *Master*."

Mephisto left Lorna's boutique in high spirits. He loved his kinky people. They were his family, the only family that accepted him as he was, with his quirks and perversions. They understood what made him tick, and shared their own vulnerable secrets so he could return that understanding to them. He was in the fantasy-fulfillment business, and he took his work seriously. It wasn't just sex. It was his life.

He stopped at an Indian eatery owned by more of his kinky friends to get some takeout for him and Molly. As he waited for the food, he thought that he really didn't know any vanilla people anymore, aside from his conservative family back east. Even before he opened Club Mephisto he'd been a party promoter, and his parties had increasingly inched to the fetish side. Like Molly, perhaps, he was born to this life. He felt genetically programmed to it, and when he was out amidst large groups of vanillas—when it really couldn't be avoided—it didn't feel right.

He returned to the club and unlocked the door, finding Molly hard at work polishing the bar top. Standing back there, he could remember her as she was then, slinging beer, mixing cocktails. Twenty-one, twenty-two years old maybe when he hired her. She had to be almost thirty now, but she looked younger than she had in her early twenties. The anger and cynicism had aged her prematurely, but it was all gone now. Seemingly.

But things in the kink world weren't always what they seemed.

He saw her eying the bag and decided to make her wait and wonder what was inside. Molly surely recognized the shop name, since Clayton was one of Lorna's biggest customers. Her imagination would probably invent much worse things than what he'd actually bought. Well, maybe not.

He took her into the kitchen, set the bag beside her on the floor, and fed her *naan* and *momos*, and Indian rice, which was tricky. Molly was lovely, taking the food so delicately from his fingertips. The rest of the time she sat and watched him, thinking about...what? What was in the bag? Thinking about him? No, when she thought about him, she looked afraid. She had that distant, dreamy-mournful look...

"What are you thinking about?"

She looked alarmed. Did she think he'd be jealous if she admitted she was daydreaming about Clayton? Maybe he would be.

"Don't worry," he said with a shrug, "you don't need to tell me. I can guess just from the look on your face. He's a lucky man to have such a devoted slave."

She blushed. "Master...I am the lucky one, to be able to serve him."

Her words came close to contradicting him, but Mephisto let it pass. "Clear these dishes away and then come join me in the play space. We're going to embark on a little training I warrant you've never experienced before."

He took the black bag with him, and went out to prep the padded table and gather some of the equipment he planned to use. Cuffs, straps, dildos, plugs, condoms for fucking her. He shed his shirt for her benefit, but left his jeans on so her own nakedness might feel more acute. Before long, Molly appeared, walking toward him with that lovely ambivalent gait of hers. *I want to come to you and obey you, but I'm afraid at the same time.* She had good reason to be.

He patted the table with a hint of a smile. Molly crossed to him and lay back on the cool black leather. As much as he wanted to throw her legs wide and start fucking her, he made himself pause to cuff her down first. Arms spread wide, wrists fastened, and then ankles fixed to stirrups. She wiggled her toes and arched her pelvis just a little. He put a hand on the inside of her thigh, using the other to inspect her pussy. She gasped softly as he thrust his fingers into her already-slick channel.

"Wet, are we?" he teased. "Yes, bondage turns me on too."

He undid his fly to release his aching dick and rolled on a condom, then pressed between her thighs. She was so hot, so tight, gripping his cock with her head thrown back, her eyes closed in concentration. He fucked her with long, pounding strokes, grinding now and again on her clit just to watch her suck in her breath and tremble.

"You haven't come since you've been here with me, girl. Have you?" he asked, mid-stroke.

She looked up at him. "I... No... You said—"

"I haven't given permission, and you've obeyed me." He twisted his hips, driving deep again. "So it's been how long for you?"

She did some mental calculations while he went on fucking her. It was so cute when they were getting fucked and trying to think at the same time. "Almost...well...two days," she finally managed. "Since the night my Master brought me here."

"And have you wanted to come since you've been here?"

"Oh...God..." He practically mounted the table, trying to find her g-spot. If her expression was any indication, he'd had success. "Oh, Master," she wailed. "I really want to come right now."

"Don't," he said. He was fucking faster now, driving her toward the very thing he denied her. Her effort not to come, her tiny whines of distress thrilled him. His climax came on him like a clap of thunder. He'd wanted to torment her longer, but not this time. He pulled out, stripped off his condom, and shot his cum over her flat stomach and up onto her breasts. She let out a soft breath of relief that became a low moan of disappointment as he did up his fly.

Mephisto laughed, rubbing his ejaculate into her skin and up around her puckered nipples. She shivered a little, her hips shifting on the table. "Don't worry," he said. "It's okay to be frustrated. Edging is frustrating. For you anyway."

She didn't seem to appreciate his attempt at humor. His lips twisted in a secret smile as he turned away to pick up a vibrator. He turned back, playing with the settings, plastering a serious, forbidding look on his face.

"Please," she begged softly. He knew she meant *Please, don't*, but he was already spreading her pussy lips, looking for that tiny, sensitive bit of flesh. He placed the tip of the vibrator right against it, on a mercifully low setting. For a while she succeeded at mind over matter. She closed her eyes and breathed evenly in and out. Her body was rigid. Fine. He wasn't in a hurry. He simply waited, moving the humming tool over and around her button until her breath sped up. Until her hips started moving in oh-so-tiny increments. Even with his recent satisfaction, his cock stirred in response.

"Please..." she whispered, gazing up at him in entreaty. He couldn't imagine how badly she must want to come.

"No begging," he said. "I'm doing this for my pleasure. This is not about you. This is about teaching you just how much control I have over you—your happiness and your misery. Do you understand?"

"Yes, Master. But...please—"

"Every time you say please, I'm going to make this even harder on you."

She turned her face away, her expression a mask of suffering. He watched her lips, her eyes, her hypnotic hips for signs she was getting too close to hold on.

When he sensed she was almost there, he turned off the vibrator and pulled it away. She whimpered like a kitten, her body all loose and trembling. He watched her breathing, waiting for it to slow. The sheen of his cum still shone between her breasts.

When she seemed calm, he flicked the toy on again. The low buzz sounded loud, almost as loud as her sigh. She turned accusing eyes on him, halting him before he even touched the vibe to her clit.

"You want to scratch my face off, don't you?"

"Master! Pleas—" She remembered too late his warning about her *pleases*. But how to make things harder on her? She was definitely a nipple-sensitive girl. He'd start there. He went and grabbed some nice cruel clover clamps connected by a chain. She watched in horror as he flicked each nipple, then closed the clamps on them. Her hips came off the table, her arms straining in their bonds. She tried desperately to wrench her legs shut as he parted her pussy again, but he was having none of that. He slapped them open and placed the vibrator right against her swollen, sex glazed clit—

Jesus Christ. Nipple sensitive all right. She came almost the second he touched her. He felt anger, frustration. Not at her, but at himself. And yes, at her. Why was she so fucking orgasmic?

"You'll have to be punished for that." He uncuffed her ankles and went for a thick leather strap. She was sobbing in quick halting gusts as he returned and lifted her legs, pushing them high in the air to expose her bottom. He gave her a hard solid crack against the juncture of ass and thighs. She screamed and almost kicked him in the head.

46

"No, no, no!" she cried as he drew his hand back again.

He continued the punishment, struggling to control her as she fought him, legs trembling. He knew it hurt her, he knew she was panicking. He held her legs against his shoulder with one hand and strapped her a few more times on her ass and the backs of her thighs. She cried and screamed "*Ow!*" and "*No!*" but to her credit, she didn't say "*Please*" again. He finally lost his patience and grabbed the chain between the clamps on her breasts, tugging it to get her attention.

"When this punishment is over, I'll stop," he said. "Until then, you will accept what you have coming to you. Do you understand me?" She caught her breath, then nodded, her face awash in tears. This had to be a hard punishment. He knew her ass still hurt from yesterday. He knew the strap felt like hell falling against her tightly stretched skin while her legs flailed in the air. Tough shit. She was a slave, and she had to take it. He grasped her ankles hard in his hands and gave her a look.

She was better for the rest of the blows. She cried, she screamed, she twisted a little, but she didn't flail, even when he delivered the last five brutal ones. Then he stopped, still holding the strap against her ass.

"Are you allowed to come without permission?" he demanded sharply.

"No, Master," she answered in a panicked voice.

"Do you deserve to come whenever you wish?"

"No, Master!"

"Who controls your pussy? Who controls your body?"

"You do, Master! Always!" He gave her one last stinger. Her wail of misery was gorgeous. Broken down. Devastated. He released her legs and left her limp and crying on the table while he went to hang up the strap. God, she was a mess. Such tears. If he

47

thought they were for show, he would have punished her further, but they were quite lovely and real.

"Stop that crying or I'll gag you."

He could tell Molly tried. She sucked in deep breaths and blew them out again. Tiny sobbing sounds still erupted from her throat now and again, but she found some place of calm. He watched her expectantly. Finally she swallowed and spoke in a tense rasp. "I'm sorry, Master. I'm sorry I displeased you. Thank you for punishing me."

"I hope you learned a lesson," he said, pinching her scarlet ass.

She choked down a cry and drew in a slow, bracing breath. "I did, Master. Thank you."

He took some tissues to her face, to the tears pooling down by her ears and the snot coming out of her nose. She babbled more apologies, more broken *thank you*'s and *oh Master*'s and *I'm sorry*'s until he finally placed his fingers over her lips.

"Enough. Just show me you've learned something. I know this might not seem important to you, but it is to me. I want you to *want*. I don't want you to achieve satisfaction. Not yet. Do you understand?"

She nodded. "Yes, Master. You want me to be frustrated and unsatisfied."

To put it bluntly, he thought, chuckling. "Yes. That's what I want," he answered out loud in an authoritative tone. He parted her legs and turned the vibrator up higher this time. He doubted she could feel anything at the moment besides the ache in her ass, but he could do this all day. He wanted her to see not only how much power he had over her, but how much he could take away. Not just her free will, but her ability to feel pleasure and respond to it in her own way. And when he finally allowed her to come...

It wasn't very long before her hips started moving again. In avoidance at first, but then in a decidedly wanton way.

"Oh, please!" she burst out. Mephisto gave her a sharp slap on the cheek.

"I said no begging. You're not trying at all to obey me," he snapped. "This would all go a lot easier for you if you'd just try. Is this how you serve your Master?"

He'd promised to make it harder for each please. He hoped she had some reserves of strength left. He grabbed a vial of ginger-based oil and returned, shaking it between his fingers. He believed she recognized it, because she started crying again. He rubbed just a fingertip's worth on her clit—enough to tease but not enough to undo all the work they'd done so far. He grabbed her face and glared at her until he had her attention. Through the pain, through the tingling and stinging of the oil, he saw her intellect there.

"Listen to me," he said slowly. "Focus. Do not come. I don't care how you manage it. I'm going to tease you, and then I'm going to stop. You restrain yourself."

"Yes, Master," she said between gasps.

He worked with her for another ten minutes, although it probably seemed like hours and hours from her suffering vantage point. He took her right to the edge two more times, and both times, with steely resolve, Molly managed not to come. With a satisfied nod of approval, he finally silenced the vibrator. A few tears of relief coursed down her cheeks, over the light mark where he'd slapped her. He ran gentle fingers up the insides of her thighs.

"I enjoyed that very much, although I doubt you did."

He removed the clamps, undid the cuffs, and put her to work licking off the mess she'd made of the upholstery. That done, he took her with him into the shower. He washed her himself, especially her pussy and clit, so she wouldn't accidentally bring herself to orgasm. *Mine. I own this for now.* Poor girl. Even as he dried her off, she still tensed and clung to him, wanting the relief he was unwilling to give her.

She would see soon enough that she wasn't getting relief anytime soon. He led her back out to the club's playroom, and opened the black bag to show her the chastity belt with its two carefully affixed metal dildos. He picked up the little vial of oil from the table and worked a thin sheen over both the rigid toys.

Molly shook her head. Cute, but pointless.

"Bend over the table."

She only hesitated a moment but that earned her another swipe of the stinging, nagging oil across her clit. Silly girl. Still trying to resist him at this point? He pinched her clit roughly and then leaned over her back with his lips at her ear. "Oh my," he breathed. "Still so slick, still so swollen."

He started working the dildos into her orifices. He had to add more oil to lubricate the one for her ass. As he finally pushed it home, she whined helplessly. "You must feel desperately horny right now," he said. "Desperately aroused."

"I do, Master," she said. "I want to come so bad."

"But you won't, will you? And now..." He smoothed the leather harness against her skin and threaded the belt around the top to hold it snug, buckling it in the back. "Now you simply won't have the ability. The oil will be enough of an irritant to keep the penetration from feeling pleasurable, and this plate will more or less put your clit out of commission. You'll have to suffer for Master's pleasure, won't you?"

"Yes, Master." Oh, God, the frustrated resignation in her voice almost had him ripping the chastity belt off to fuck her again. No, he had to show control. This was a control moment, not a selfish-impromptu-fuck moment. It was time to lock her down.

"Look at me," he said, tipping her head back. "I see no more reason for you to talk to me, only to obey. You can obey without speaking. So unless I ask you a direct question from now on, I want no words."

"But...please Master, may I ask one more question?"

"One more."

"Must I be completely silent?"

"Silent? No, girl. I said no words, not no noise." Mephisto shrugged. "Feel free to scream, whine, or whimper as needed. I actually quite enjoy hearing you make those sounds."

"Thank you, Mas—" she started to say, until he silenced her with a finger. And that was that. No more voice. He'd miss it, but he liked the control more.

The Third Day

Mephisto loved the smell of women. He loved their softness, their mystery. He loved the grace of a truly submissive woman. But sometimes he liked the roughness of a man...and there was only one man who would have dared crawl into his bed at four in the morning. Jamie.

Mephisto turned over, half asleep, and groped in his bedside drawer for a condom. He wrestled Jamie onto his stomach and leaned hard on his shoulders while he penetrated him. "Oh, God, Mephisto," Jamie whined. "That fucking hurts." Mephisto clamped a hand over his mouth and drove in to the hilt. Jamie was a brat. Fucking him was kind of like fucking a tornado, but Mephisto enjoyed that about him.

Tonight though, Mephisto was tired. He grabbed a fistful of Jamie's blond hair and pressed his face down into the pillow until he stopped tossing around. "Good boy," Mephisto crooned. "Lie still, quietly, and let me take your asshole."

Mephisto wasn't sure if he made him be quiet as a power-and-control thing, or so he wouldn't wake up Molly. Not that Mephisto cared if his slave missed out on sleep, but she might be alarmed to find a large, unknown stranger in the room with them. The power-and-control factor was pretty nice too. Jamie was usually very vocal, especially bottoming, but now he shuddered under Mephisto in silence, his mouth impeded by Mephisto's hard palm. "Good boy," Mephisto said again. "Obedient fucking slut."

There weren't many men who got Mephisto going. When he was with Jamie, his body responded to the dichotomy of Jamie's power paired with submission. It was a heady mix. It was one thing to make a woman submit. With Mephisto's strength and stature, he could theoretically force compliance from a woman. With Jamie, whose strength matched Mephisto's, compliance had to be granted, and it *was* granted...barely. It was the "barely" that got Mephisto hot.

By the time morning arrived, Mephisto was hard again. Molly was probably awake and getting an eyeful. Mephisto didn't care, didn't even look her way. He sat up on the edge of the bed, fisting his cock and eying Jamie. "Suck me," he ordered in a tired, impatient growl.

The muscular man crawled between Mephisto's legs and ran his tongue up his cock and around the bulbous head. Then he shifted and took him deep, with warm, shudder-inducing pressure. Jesus, Mephisto adored women, he really did, but no one sucked cock like a man. The pleasure built fast, buzzed and pulsed in his balls. Jamie pumped his dick and then deep throated him over and over.

Mephisto loved when Jamie blew through town.

He heard a sound from Molly's cage and turned to her. He could hardly focus, but he saw her eyes were wide. She was watching intently. The idea of that turned him on so much he grabbed Jamie's head and practically choked him with his thrusts. Mephisto came less than a minute later, spewing in the back of his friend's throat. Mephisto fell back on the bed, stretching and basking in the afterglow of the powerful orgasm. "We have an audience," he said, nodding in Molly's direction.

Jamie turned to look at her. "Who is she?"

"Someone I'm watching for the week. Slavegirl. More of a fuck doll, but it's her Master's tastes."

Mephisto let her out and took off the harness since he'd be in direct control of her for the next few hours. It wasn't until they were halfway through breakfast that he realized she was in a bad mood. Her back was ramrod straight, and her eyes avoided his even when he fed her. Jealousy? That would be flattering. Frustration over the orgasm denial? More likely.

"So who does she belong to?" Jamie asked as he tore into his second omelet.

"Friend of mine. You don't know him."

"She's quiet."

"She's not allowed to talk."

Jamie's eyes widened. "For how long?"

"For as long as I like. Maybe all week." Mephisto shrugged. "She's used to control. She needs it." Although she didn't look so happy just then. Come to think of it, Jamie looked a little cranky too. Battle of the jealous fuck toys. Mephisto had a momentary comic impulse to set them loose in the dungeon together with a couple of weapons and see who survived. Jamie was strong, but Molly was little and quick. Clayton kept her in good shape. Mephisto pictured her straddling Jamie with a knife at his jugular and a howl of victory on her lips.

"What are you laughing at?" Jamie asked.

Mephisto shook his head. "Nothing. Finish eating and clean up the dishes. I have to harness her again if we're going to go out."

Mephisto led her back to his bedroom and pulled her into his lap on the bed. "I wonder what's the matter with my pouty little sex slave this morning," he said lightly. He turned her so her back was to his front, and then spread her thighs. There was an infinitesimal moment of resistance, quickly quelled. He traced over her pubic lips, her slick, swollen clit. She pressed her head back against his shoulder with a moan.

"Hmm, she's turned on, so she must be enjoying herself," he murmured. "What a mystery."

He teased her a little more, drawing her juices up from between her legs to draw circles around her nipples and breasts. Each touch, each caress was met with a whimper or sigh.

"No, I just don't understand it," he whispered against her ear. "It's too bad she's not permitted to talk. She could just tell me what the problem was. That...perhaps...she really wanted to come, but Master won't let her. Or perhaps she's jealous of Master's friend, who gets all the hard cock he wants and gets to come too, all over Master's bedsheets." He nipped at her delicate earlobe. "It seems so unfair. You know, I jacked him off while I fucked him. I wanted him to come. But you don't get to come, do you?"

He put a hand over her mouth before she slipped up and replied. "Oh, and you don't get to talk either. Poor girl. Ah, well." He put her back in the harness—without the dildos—and leashed her to the foot of his bed. She looked up at him in resignation. "Be a good girl," he said.

With his slave squared away, Mephisto accompanied Jamie to a photo shoot and interview for a local magazine. Jamie was part of a Seattle-grown band gone big. Mephisto had known Jamie for years, since college. Jamie was a great musician and a charismatic performer. He certainly deserved his success, although, less than a year into it, he was already jaded by fame. Mephisto watched in amusement as hordes of female groupies swarmed Jamie outside his hotel. He thought of Molly back at Club Mephisto, kneeling beside his bed. Had she recognized Jamie? Most likely not. He doubted Jamie's brand of progressive funk rock got a lot of play on Clayton's sound system.

After a late lunch he and Jamie went back to the club to play some more. They got out the heavy toys, whips and anal hooks and floggers. Jamie was a sick masochist, and Mephisto enjoyed beating the crap out of someone who was really, really hard to break down. No fragility there...just an able male body begging *more, more, more. Is that all you got?* Mephisto worked over his friend until Jamie just about reached his limit, until Mephisto's own cock was bursting for satisfaction. He dragged Jamie back to the bedroom.

In the frenzy of their violent scening he'd forgotten about Molly kneeling there beside his bed. He wondered what she'd made of all the noises filtering back from the dungeon. She was staring at his cock and practically drooling. God, he was so worked up. He leaned over the bed and signaled Jamie to fuck him. Jamie rolled on a condom and added plenty of lube. He had a big fucking dick, and even when Mephisto bottomed to him, Mephisto was still the top. Jamie knew better than to brutalize him.

Mephisto grunted as Jamie's cock breached his ass. The sliding burn set him on fire, unleashed some carnal violence in him. Jamie's tentative hands rested on his hips and Mephisto felt a sudden animal impulse to fuck something else while he was being fucked.

"Girl!" Molly jumped at his feet. He jerked her leash, unwrapping it with shaking hands. "Up. Go get a condom. Now."

She ran to get one and skittered back, her eyes on his jutting cock. Behind him, Jamie was pulling back and driving deep again, clutching at Mephisto's hips, groaning to hold back his own orgasm. He knew better than to come before Mephisto.

"Lay on the bed," Mephisto ordered, grabbing the condom from Molly, ripping open the wrapper, and rolling it down his length. He was so worked up, even that contact was excruciating. He cursed under his breath, working the buckles of her chastity belt and yanking it off. He drove inside her, into her wet, tight, needy center, levering himself over her with his hands braced on the bed. Behind him, Jamie thrust harder, faster, running his hands up Molly's thighs.

It was a glorious fuckfest. Mephisto's anus clenched around the cock in his ass while he drove recklessly into his slave, and each movement, each stroke brought a greater intensity to the joining. Jamie's groans were peaking, and Mephisto's whole body vibrated with a pleasure that felt dangerous. He ground his teeth and put his hands over Jamie's on Molly's thighs. She was panting, her breasts bouncing and her head thrown back as he jolted her against the bed.

"Don't come," he grunted, pinching her nipple. "You. Girl. You don't come."

He barely caught her nod before he lost it, ramming her hard, spilling himself inside her pussy in white hot pulses of release. Behind him, Jamie bucked and practically knocked him over onto Molly as he climaxed. Mephisto pushed him back and they fell to the floor in a grapple that ended in a long, lingering kiss. When he finally got up to strap Molly back into her chastity harness, her eyes were shimmering with tears. What would she say if he let her speak?

He thought it was kinder not to let her speak at all.

* * * * *

Later that evening, Mephisto fed Molly, and then he and Jamie went out bar crawling. They eventually ended up at a scruffy Irish bar on the east side of town. Mephisto chuckled as Jamie eased gingerly onto the bar stool beside him.

"You wanted to play hard," Mephisto said with a shrug.

"Fuck you. You know I have a fucking show to do tomorrow."

"Poor baby."

"You're such a ruthless bastard."

"And you love me that way."

Jamie raised a glass to him and took a deep drink of the Irish pint, then put it down on the bar with a bang. "Don't know how you can stand to play with those little girlies though. And fuck them," he added with a shudder.

"That's because you're a gay man," Mephisto said drily. "I have half a mind to make you fuck her later."

"I couldn't do it."

"You could if I ordered you to, my friend. Or would that be too ruthless? Technique wouldn't matter," he added with a smirk. "She's not allowed to come."

Jamie smiled and leaned his head on his hand. "You're a sick fuck. Very nice. She can't *ever* come?"

"Oh, eventually I'll let her come. That's the whole point of it, to get her worked up to the point where she's out of her mind, and then when she's finally allowed to come..." Mephisto threw his hands out in an explosive movement. "Complete craziness. It's fantastic."

After a moment of silence, Jamie said, "So...when you finally settle down with someone, I guess it'll be some slavey girl like her."

"When I finally 'settle down?' Since when can you not hold your alcohol?"

"Ah." Jamie shook his head. "You'll settle down one day. You say you won't, but you will."

"Fuck you." Mephisto laughed, but his thoughts went to Clayton. For many years, even before Mephisto was established, Clayton had been a Seattle scene regular. A party guy. A slut Master, until he found his Molly. Clayton had settled down with her within the year. "Who do you think I should settle down with?" Mephisto asked his friend.

Jamie winked at him. "Me, of course."

Mephisto chuckled. "When you grow a nice set of tits." *Like Molly's.* Would he settle down with a slavegirl like Molly someday? The idea of settling down with anyone was so alien to Mephisto he couldn't even picture how it might work. Jamie had found any number of "true loves" in his life, all of which generally burned out within a year. Mephisto watched his friend fall apart after all of them and thought that was infinitely worse than remaining alone. But years from now, when Mephisto was in his mid forties...his mid fifties... When he was lying in bed, dying, who would be at his side? Clayton knew who would be at his side. A beautiful devoted slavegirl.

Maybe. Would Molly remain Clayton's slave years from now? Forever? Would she ever stop wanting to be a slave? That was the type of thought that took his breath away. Consensual slavery could end at any time, since consent was the only thing that made "slavery" okay. "Jesus," Mephisto muttered into his beer.

Jamie was hiding under a cap and tinted glasses, but it wasn't long before they were found out. The Irish band hammering away in the corner launched into a cover of one of Jamie's songs and he was obliged to sing a few before they could slip away. By then there was a crowd outside and they had to escape into a cab. They took a circuitous ride around the city so no one would follow them back to the club. Mephisto thought about Molly as Jamie groped him through his pants. Would she ever stop wanting to be a slave? What would she become then? Would her value be more, or less? To Clayton, to the world? To Mephisto?

Mephisto felt himself falling into a black mood. Back at the club, he did force Jamie to fuck Molly, an act both slaves found distasteful, although Jamie was sustained through the copulation by Mephisto's big hard dick in his ass. Molly didn't look at either of them as she drifted in deep slave usage mode, and Mephisto didn't force her to tune in. Instead he drilled Jamie until his gay friend came, so he would have to live with the fact he'd fucked a woman to completion. Mephisto's own orgasm wasn't as powerful as the last. It was tempered by lingering irritation, so when Jamie turned to him and lied through his teeth that Molly had had an orgasm, Mephisto decided to play along. He turned hard, accusing eyes on her.

Molly was devastated, shaking her head with all the insistence she could muster. Her lips trembled helplessly with the need to defend herself. When Mephisto dragged her into the dungeon, she finally blurted out, "He's lying! I don't know why, but he's ly—"

Mephisto clapped a hand over her mouth and pulled her close. "You're on speech restriction, bad girl. Who gave you permission to talk?"

It was a cruel, cruel thing to do, but he was allowed to be cruel to her. She burst into tears as Jamie helped Mephisto cuff her to the

St. Andrew's Cross with her back exposed. What a lying piece of shit Jamie was, but his petty jealousies were one more trial to lie at Molly's willing feet. There was a certain melodrama to it all. She collapsed at the first lick of the lash, her legs going from under her. He'd seen her take whips just fine from Clayton, so her struggling and misery undoubtedly stemmed from the injustice of her situation. Mephisto knew he should be beating Jamie right now, not Molly. Jamie knew it, and Molly too. But sometimes, power exchange was about poking a cornered animal until you found the point where it snapped.

"Up," Mephisto ordered, landing another one on the outside of her flank. She struggled, she fought, but Mephisto continued, determined to subdue her. After twenty minutes or so he had Jamie turn her around. The look she gave the man...such vitriol. Such hatred in those eyes. Mephisto paused, entranced. There she was. That was the Molly he remembered, right there.

She was still there.

He lifted the whip to her again, tormenting licks and stripes. It was the continued assault that broke her down, not the pain of any one strike. She screamed, she sobbed, jerking in her bonds as he flicked fiery pain on belly, thighs, nipples, breasts. In between screams, she sobbed, and then she fell silent, closing her eyes. Finally, submission. But he didn't want it, not now, when he'd seen the other Molly hiding in there.

"Look at me!"

Her eyes snapped open, moved to Jamie and fixed on him with that same terrible anger. Leave it to Jamie to get aroused by that. He was fisting his cock, enjoying the violence. But he'd given up his last chance at pleasure with this stunt.

"Look at me," Mephisto barked again to Molly.

61

She stared in his eyes and held his gaze as he flicked the whip again, a sting on each breast. She'd cried so much her face was ashen, glowing. Then he saw her relax and let it all go. He let it go too, and let the whip fall still. Enough. He went to the wall to hang it up and get a set of clamps. When he came back she was watching him, not angrily, not sadly. Just resigned. He wiped her face with his palms and subdued the impulse to kiss her. Instead he applied the clamps to his slave's tits and clitoris with businesslike detachment and left her hanging there.

"Come," he said to Jamie. His friend loped behind him to the bedroom. Once inside, Mephisto took a swing at him that sent him to the floor. Jamie hissed in protest, but wisely stayed down.

"Don't ever, ever lie to me again," Mephisto said.

Jamie held his face, staring up at him with the same anger Molly had turned on him before. "Who gives a shit?" he said. "It seemed to serve your purposes. She's just a fucking slavegirl, right?"

"Never lie to me again," Mephisto repeated. "Whether it serves my purposes or not. It makes you look small, Jamie. Really small. And I don't like you that way."

Later, after Jamie left, Mephisto went to face her, his silent martyr. His miserable slave. As he stood and watched her, she started to cry again, horrible emotionless tears. She was still in there. Molly. The old Molly. That was the force, the power she subsumed to serve the man she loved. Mephisto wanted to go on his knees before her. He wanted to worship her.

He wanted her. He wanted that depth of devotion for himself.

"It's hard, girl, isn't it?" he asked quietly.

He took off the clamps and tried to feed her, but she was too upset. He didn't have much appetite either, although he made her drink a little water, sip by halting sip. So many tears. She'd be dehydrated. He bathed her, checking over the whip marks. A few had drawn blood, and he treated them with antibiotic cream.

He put her to bed in the cage without the harness and locked the padlock with feelings of euphoria and yet devastation. He watched her until she fell asleep—it was perhaps three minutes—and then he still sat and watched her chest rise and fall in sleep, his hands threaded through the bars. *Molly, I'm sorry for all the lies. The dishonesty and jealousy. Jamie's and mine.*

The Fourth Day

Mephisto let her sleep. She'd earned it. When she woke, there was a new tension between them. A loss of trust, but a capitulation too. Yes, she couldn't trust him, but yes, she had to obey him anyway. Of course it upset her, but that was okay.

He fucked her on the floor right outside the cage, a re-orienting and another opportunity to frustrate her libido. The cruel scene of the night before hadn't dampened her need the least bit. She'd been wet as the ocean when he'd clamped her clit.

She was still wet now, her eyes begging and hopeless all at once. After breakfast he edged her again, fucked her ass for a long time, and then locked her down tight for the day, dildos and all.

The orgasm denial was like an experiment, Molly the only subject. What was going to happen? How far could he push her? Would she eventually rebel? Mephisto realized that's all he really was, a mad scientist of humanity. He wanted to understand people, like that might bring him some peace, some feeling of accomplishment. It was a quest for knowledge that never ended.

By lunchtime he wanted to fuck Molly again. She was a compulsion, an addiction. He wanted to be thrusting his dick in her all the time. He pushed her to her knees in the kitchen and fucked her face and Jesus goddamnit, how he ached to come in her mouth. Not in the condom, but deep in her luscious throat. He texted Clayton while she served him. Missed a few letters. *Moly is fine. blowig me now.* Clayton would get the general idea. Afterward, he held her in his lap and fed her, enjoying her tremors and the sexual frustration communicated in the tenseness of her legs. When they finished eating, she laid her head back against his shoulder and he held her, rather than pushing her down to the floor. He slipped fingers down the front of her harness to tease her pussy. He thought he could have sat like this with her for hours. He turned her head to lick and kiss her mouth. She had tiny little worry lines between her eyes.

"What is it, girl? Forgot your name? It's Molly," he teased, but she didn't smile. He kissed her again, more deeply, stroking a fingertip across her clit at the same time. She moaned into his mouth, a small, half-hearted reaction. He pulled away and she hid her face against his neck. She was struggling, spiraling down. *Molly, Molly, don't forget who you are.*

"I know a lot about you, girl," he said, rubbing his chin against her soft dark curls. "You'd probably be surprised. I know your maiden name was Molly Grace Belden, and your married name is Molly Grace Copeland. I know your birthday is April seventh, and that you were born and raised in Bloomington. I know you have an environmental science degree from IU." With every word, she seemed to draw up tighter and tighter. "I know something else about you," he said. "I know you didn't really come yesterday."

He waited for a reaction, any bodily reaction, but she only turned her head a little more into the curve of his shoulder. He cupped her pussy and sighed. He didn't like her withdrawal, her surrender. It was too weak. He nudged her back so she couldn't hide her face.

"You're wondering why I punished you when I knew?" he asked. "I was punishing you for speaking, for protesting. For your tone. And because it pleases me to hurt you sometimes just because I can. Just because I enjoy pushing you to your limits and watching the breakdown." His fingers moved again on her clit. How much she must hate him... He laughed softly and brought his fingers to her nose for a moment so she could breathe in her feminine scent. Her needy scent. "It's the same thing with the orgasm denial, kitten. I enjoy watching the build up, seeing how far I can tease and wrap you around my fingers. How much I can make you dance. The denial is just a tool for winding you up so I can watch you writhe and wriggle for me."

She pressed her face back against his neck, making a small distressed sound. She moved her hips, just a little, but he didn't stop his lazy torment. His finger slid across her taut little button and down into the cleft of her pussy. He tightened his arm on her waist when she moved her hips and started to tremble.

"You see?" He chuckled against her ear. "Not letting you come...it's like the rubber band on those little wooden airplane toys: You twist and twist them until you can't twist them anymore, then you let it go and watch them fly around the room."

She pulled away from him then, the first real sign of rebellion. He liked it, but at the same time, he had to put it down. He drew his hand out of her harness and grabbed her face.

"You have to trust me, girl. I think you don't trust me. I know we haven't had a lot of time together, but I'm being careful. Perhaps you don't see it, but I am." He reached for her waist and tightened the harness. Enough cuddle time. "Listen, I want you to really clean and straighten up the play space today. There's a big party tomorrow. A private party. An orgy," he finally clarified, laughing at the sudden hope that spread across her face. Yes, it would have been the perfect occasion to release her from orgasm restriction. But—

"No, you won't yet be permitted to come," he said to put down her false hope. "I'll let everybody know. And girl, you won't want to be punished in front of everyone if you screw up. So beware. It might be best if we did a little more edging practice tonight." Mephisto pinched her nipples until she flinched, and then slapped her breasts. "You know, I might not permit you to come at all until you're returned to your Master. What a gift that would be for him, no? To return you absolutely wild with horniness. Maybe he'd find he liked you that way. I could give him lots of advice about an effective denial program. And that harness is going home with you and him. Hopefully he'll make good use of it."

Her look of distress was priceless. Even better—her attempt to hide the depth of her despair behind her equivocal slavey face.

"Nice try, kitten. But everything you think and feel is written on your face, clear as daylight." He slapped her ass. "Now get going. I better not find one speck of dust."

* * * * *

He left her out in the dungeon, cleaning. He had professional teams come in to do the real cleaning, of course, but she didn't know that. She worked so hard, as if she alone was responsible for Club Mephisto putting its best foot forward. Silly, earnest girl. If she saw the real mess that was left behind, the mess that was cleaned up while she slept in her snug little cage—the semen, the condoms, the sweat, the lube—she'd probably never recover.

67

Mephisto went in the back, stripped and showered and decided not to get dressed again. He lay back on his bed and dialed Clayton's cell.

"How is she today?" Clayton asked as a greeting.

Mephisto laughed. "You sound about as tired as she does."

"Ah, my poor slave. Long night?"

"The long night's tonight. We're hosting a party. Molly can attend, I suppose?"

"If you think she'll enjoy it. Or not enjoy it," he added with a chuckle. "Is she still on lockdown?"

"Yes."

"Any slip ups?"

Mephisto paused. "No. But there was an interesting episode last night. Long story, but she ended up with some whip marks. Nothing that won't be healed by tomorrow."

Clayton was quiet a moment. "She has delicate skin. She's more delicate than she looks."

"I'm sorry. I didn't mean to."

"Accidents happen," he said tightly. "How is she otherwise?"

Shit. Clayton was angry as hell. "She's fine. She's trying hard to be good. It's difficult for her. She's not used to me."

"And how are you?" Clayton asked with his usual incisive sharpness.

Mephisto sighed and stared at the ceiling. "Let's just say I'm not used to her either. I'm trying to get through to what... I'm trying to..."

There was a lengthy silence on the line before Clayton spoke. "You know, Mephisto, I really appreciate you doing this. I think it's important, but it's messy too. I know that, but I trust you. You do what you think you have to do. Molly will survive, and you will, and I will too."

Mephisto hung up with Clayton and tried to refocus on the things he needed to do. Emails, contacts. Equipment to be procured for the club. He ordered dinner in and only then reconnected with Molly, feeding her at his feet. He would miss this when she was gone, these times feeding her. He did it with other slaves now and again, for play, but he'd become used to having Molly there at every meal, perched so prettily on her knees, taking only what he saw fit to give her. If he watched her closely enough as they ate, he could see the small signs she gave, that she was still hungry, or that she was full. Now and again she shifted in her chastity harness. Those signs were crystal clear. Still horny and frustrated.

After dinner Mephisto went back to his desk to roll through the last of the correspondence and bills, club duties made somewhat less tedious by Molly's hot, skilled mouth sucking his cock under the desktop. He half-focused on her, her pleasurable ministrations background music for what he had to admit was a very cushy life. Ten minutes went by. Fifteen. She started to flag and he slapped her cheek lightly to re-engage her. Her body was warm against his legs. He looked down to see her moving her hips in a sinuous dance of aroused need, the black straps of her harness standing out in stark contrast on her light skin. The sight of it, paired with the pressure of her eager throat, finally nudged him over the edge into a long pulsing orgasm.

His body relaxed, spent. She took off his condom and a few moments later he felt her curling up under the desk at his feet. The night Clayton had brought her, she'd done the same thing, and he'd watched, charmed. It did feel nice. He ran his fingers through her hair, drifting, barely attending to his work. He let himself imagine yet again what it might be like to have a devoted slave like Molly at his service, day in and day out.

He wasn't accomplishing anything. He shut his laptop and made Molly crawl beside him back to the bedroom. He checked her tiny nicks from the night before and was relieved to find them all healing nicely. He released her from the harness and cleaned her up in the shower, using it as an excuse to explore every inch of her. She clung to him, her hair turning glossy and black under the warm spray. He enjoyed the way she openly ogled him as he washed her, and offered her the soap with a half-smile when he was done.

She smiled back. Perhaps a little of her misery was lifting. She took her time, caressing and kneading his muscles, giving him the side-eye every so often. Such invitation. Reckless thing. He stopped her when she reached for his cock and took her fingers in his, kissing her once, twice. She shivered in his arms, even in the steam of the shower. He pulled her closer just to feel her small, lithe body against his. The water slid over her velvet skin as he kissed her again, running his hands all over the beautiful shape of her. Men were fun once in a while, but they weren't soft and curvy like this. He squeezed her sore cheeks and she moaned. He slipped a finger into her wet pussy and she skittered closer, going up on her toes. Her begging look...my God.

His cock was about to burst.

He shut off the water and gave her an assessing smile. "You horny little piece of ass. You wanton sex doll. Keep a hold of yourself." He toweled her off and pushed her in the direction of the bedroom. "On the bed, face down. No, wait a minute."

He went ahead of her, opened a drawer and pulled out a folded drop cloth. He spread it over the bed sheets, right in the center. Wax was a bitch to get out of sheets. "Okay, now," he said, drawing back. "Face down."

Molly did as she was told, although she looked a little leery.

"Arms out, legs spread," he said.

He bound her first, wrists and ankles, with leather cuffs. He left her just enough room to squirm. That would be important. As she watched, he moved around the room collecting all the things he wanted to torment her with—a white taper candle, cinnamon lubricant, a riding crop, and her nemesis, a slim silver vibrator.

He chuckled at her tiny, helpless whimper. Looking for pity? Fat chance.

"Don't worry, kitten," he said, kneeling beside her on the bed. "You'll enjoy this very much. Well, parts of it." He took his time, working a thin sheen of the sting-y lube onto the base of the candle in her line of vision. "Arch your hips up."

She offered her asshole for the candle's insertion compliantly enough, although she flinched when he struck the match. "Be still," he warned when she tried to turn. He placed a hand on the small of her back to hold her steady as he lit the candle. "I want absolutely no movement. At least for a moment."

She obeyed, clenching her fists. He stroked her back lightly. Her ass cheeks were tensing, no doubt from the nagging lube. When the candle had burned for a few moments and a little pool of wax built up, he pinched her on the inside of her thigh, right on a sore spot. She yelped and twisted, and then she screeched as liquid wax sprayed across her cheeks. He put his hand on her back to calm her. "Still."

He let her think a moment, gather her wits as the pain of the hot wax subsided. This game was simple and really fun. If Molly stayed still, the wax pooling beneath the flame slid harmlessly down the side of the candle. If she moved, it splashed across her skin. So her role was to be as still as possible.

Mephisto's role, as a sadist, was to make it impossible for her to stay still.

71

He released her and she wisely lay completely dormant. Barely breathing. He picked up the crop and saw her brace. With a flick of his wrist he caught her hard across the back of a thigh. She jerked and moaned as wax spilled over the top of the other leg. Her hands clenched in her bonds and she shook her head, then looked back at him. If looks could kill...

He cracked her on the left cheek, leaving a nice red rectangle and prompting an explosion of liquid wax across her right buttock. She tensed and threw her head back with a desperate sound.

He put a hand on the small of her back again, soothing her. "This is great, isn't it?" he asked. The buzz of the vibrator drowned out her faint answering whine. "Now, this will be even more fun."

Mephisto carefully parted her pussy lips until he located her swollen clit. He only teased at first, keeping the tingle on low. She let out a soft shuddery sigh and he knew she thought she had this. But as a few more moments passed, she understood that he wasn't just going to edge her. He was going to make her pull away, and God help her if she didn't pull away fast enough.

As the minutes ticked by, a low moan started deep in her chest. She was so rigid, so tense. He thought she'd be stiff and sore tomorrow from tensing up her muscles for so long. Her ass still clenched around the candle, which was burning ever closer to her skin. She whined, pleading in the only way she could for his mercy, but he ignored her, continuing his patient assault on her horny, sex-starved little clit.

A moment later, she jerked her hips, pulling away in a convulsive movement and making a horrible sad sound at the same time. No orgasm, only hot drops of wax. Ouch.

"Good girl," he said, brushing a hand down her back before pinning her still again. "Such an obedient slave. Your Master is pleased."

Was Clayton ever this cruel to her? Mephisto was sure he sometimes was. He let her rest and then fired the vibrator up again and made her endure the long dreadful climb to the apex she wasn't permitted to reach, the long dreadful climb that would only bring more and more pain. He did it three, four more times. The last time she burst into tears. He was pushing it. He relented and turned off the vibrator, blew out the candle which had ended up being the perfect length. Perfect slave-torturing burn time.

He undid the cuffs holding her ankles and then knelt on the bed behind her, rolling on a condom. He slid his knees under her and lifted her pelvis. Her ass still clenched around the candle...her pussy was slick, shiny...unsatisfied. Her clit jutted out as if to beg for attention. He avoided touching it, instead driving his cock into her pussy. He fucked her quick and rough, his fingers scraping at the wax. Occasionally he twisted the candle, driving it deeper in her ass and pulling it out again. He would have liked to fuck her a long time, but her clasping pussy and straining ass had him rutting without thought, without control. Within minutes he was driving deep in her with his last frenzied thrusts, and then satisfaction was exploding out of him. The satisfaction of mastering her. Hurting her and thrilling her. Not letting her come.

He stayed still in her afterward, toying with the candle and stroking her back. She was relaxed now, overdosed on stimulation maybe, to the point where she seemed on the verge of sleep. He let her drowse as he rose to discard his condom, and then took her into the bathroom to peel the wax off all her luscious curves and clean her up again. She was dazed, pliable. Subspacey. "I'm very proud of you, kitten," he said, pressing a kiss to her forehead. It had been her hardest challenge yet. Not only had she been denied her own pleasure, but she'd been forced to hurt herself in the course of doing so. At first it had angered her, clearly, but by the end she'd given in. Not for her. For him, for his pleasure.

He decided to let her sleep beside him in his bed that night as a reward. He didn't even put on the chastity belt, only used the wrist cuffs to fix her hands out of reach of her aching tingly parts. When he pulled her back against him, she melted into his arms. A conquered content slavegirl, sleepy and soft beside him...

Maybe it wasn't her he was rewarding. Maybe it was him.

The Fifth Day

It felt strange to wake up beside her. Mephisto felt a delight tempered by guilt, like he was harboring stolen property. He had a thousand things to do, but he lay still beside her instead and studied her, the curve of her ear, the way her hair curled over her shoulder as she slept. She fit against him so naturally. In this quiet moment of repose he felt a strange psychic connection to her, but it was an unfounded one. That was the problem with him and Molly. Mephisto knew her to a point, and she knew him, but there were too many obscuring walls between them to really connect.

At any rate, she wasn't his to connect with. But now, with her helpless in sleep and snuggled against him, it was easy to forget. It was just the two of them in that moment, unexpectedly and tenuously tied together, rather than Master and slave. Master and slave was preferable because it was simple, clearly defined. There could be no misunderstandings, no mess. But then it struck Mephisto that it was also a closed path. Stalemate. A loss of possibility wrapped in a collar and made to obey.

75

Ugh, such thoughts. He woke her, fed her, and returned her to his room so he could go out to the gym before the orgy. He had to work off some of the agitation she stirred in him. Rather than leave her harnessed, he bent her over and lubed up a large butt plug. She watched him with mute dread. Of course she didn't want it, but it was for her own good.

"I know many of my guests will want to use your ass tonight, kitten," he said, kicking her legs apart and landing a couple sharp slaps on her ass cheeks. "Open for Master."

It was hard to get the plug in, but then she was so little. In, out, easing forward and back until the thick toy finally slid in and her body unwound with relief. If she was his, he would have worked on her ass every day until she lost her tension, her panic at each insertion. Then again, it was kind of fun to have to force his way each time. Ah... No, no time to fuck her now. He'd leave her to reflect on the fullness of her ass and hopefully do some squirming while he was away. It had been three days now since she'd been allowed to orgasm, three days since she'd been allowed to speak. Three days of silent helplessness, broken only by her one outburst at his injustice.

"Here," he said, pointing to the place at the foot of the bed where he could monitor her on the camera. She knelt down, gingerly settling back on her heels while he gathered his keys and cell phone. He went to his bookshelf and grabbed a lurid little erotica title sure to have her clenching her thighs together. He placed it on the bed beside her with a smile.

"Some reading for you," he said. "Don't want you to be bored."

Mephisto felt a lot better once he got to the gym. He worked his ass off, losing himself in honing his body. Narcissism, now that was a simple thing. He supposed, in some way, he had to believe himself entitled to the dominion he lorded over others. Or maybe he was just an egotistical, selfish prick. He certainly enjoyed the thought of Molly sitting back at his home next to his bed, her aching pussy weeping for completion, her ass stretched out by his plug.

He'd have to let her go in three days. Less than three days. He would need to start letting go of her soon.

Later. He'd worry about all that later. He did some laps in the pool and showered, imagining Molly freaking out from horniness bent over the erotica book. But when he returned, she was sitting just as calm and unruffled as could be. He felt a moment of rage, thinking she might have masturbated, but then he noticed the book sitting exactly where he'd placed it on the bed.

He decided to give her the benefit of the doubt. Maybe she'd already finished and replaced it. "I expected to find you reading. What did you think of the book?"

He could see understanding dawn. Yes, she was supposed to read. He'd been fantasizing about her frustration all afternoon. "You didn't read it? At all?" She bowed her head at the irritation in his voice. He stalked toward her. "Why do you think I left it there beside you? As I said, it was reading for you. Reading I expected you to do."

She was already cringing as he sat on the edge of the bed and reached for her, throwing her down over his lap. Bad little slave, to circumvent all his fun with her self-protective choices. He lectured her sharply, each word punctuated with a similarly sharp smack of his hand against her ass.

"How forward of you, slave, to just assume a choice. I don't give you choices. I give you instructions." *Smack. Smack. Smack.* He pressed the plug deeper in her ass, then spanked her again even harder so she whimpered and strained against him. "I give the instructions in this relationship. You follow them. If I take the time to pick out a fucking book and give it to you, you fucking—" *Smack.* "Read." *Smack.* "It. Don't you?" *Smack. Smack. Smack.*

She cried, but she didn't struggle. She understood how badly she'd fucked up, taking her punishment with the stoicism of the guilty. But oh, how she cried, and the harder she cried, the harder he knew he had to punish her. With a growl, he stood and pushed her facedown over the bed. He fumbled with the buckle of his belt, yanking it out of his jeans and doubling it over. He leaned his knee on the small of her back to hold her down and then brought the belt across her ass full force. She wailed miserably, eying the book still lying on the bed right near her face.

He lashed her again, and then again, the blows resounding loudly in the room, joined by her pitiful cries and his own heavy breaths. "From now on, you don't do what you decide you prefer. You do what I tell you to do." *Whack!* "Open the book, now, and start reading."

Molly scrambled to get the book. She opened it with trembling fingers and tried in vain to stammer out the title and the author's name, then cried out as the belt fell again. Her voice, unused for so long, sounded scratchy and thick. She tripped over syllables, trying to form the words.

"Louder, so I can hear you!" He brought the belt singing down over the red marks from the previous blows, and she jumped under the pressure of his knee.

She started over again, trying to enunciate through her whimpers. She stammered through the opening paragraphs as her tears dampened the page. He continued to beat her until he thought she'd had enough, until her ass was deep and uniformly red. He lifted his knee from her back and flung the belt down beside her.

"Keep reading," he barked when she paused. "Read the whole damn thing. Out loud. Don't move until you're done. You deserve worse, but I want my guests to have a chance to mark you at the party," he said with a final frustrated slap to her rear. He stormed back out to the club and paced around doing mindless tasks until he calmed down. Not that he'd been out of control. She'd disobeyed and he'd punished her, which was certainly within his rights. He'd punished her to the degree she needed to feel adequately corrected.

No, the problem was that he felt too invested in her. Her failures felt like his failures. He wanted her to be perfect, just as Clayton trained her to be perfect, just as Molly herself endeavored to be perfect. He sat and had a drink, listening to her voice struggling through the story. Well, at least now she'd gotten her chance to speak, perhaps not in the way she would have wished. As she was whimpering her way through the last chapter, Mephisto went back to her. She was still bent over the bed, her ass fading from scarlet to a dull shade of reddish purple. He asked her a few questions about the book to be sure she'd actually taken it in—not that arousal was very likely for her at this point.

"Put the book on the shelf, and then return to kneel here before me," he said, going for a condom.

She limped over to put up the book, then returned and fell to her knees, her eyes down, head bowed. He took her face in his hands and thrust into her mouth, not being gentle. She tried hard to please him, to make amends for her slip up. Over time, he decreased the violence of his thrusts, even stroked a hand over the sheen of her night-dark hair. The sharp pleasure of his orgasm arrived with a sense of mellowing, almost fondness for her.

He tipped her face up. She looked like she might speak, plead or apologize, but he silenced her. "No. No talking. I don't want it.

Just listen to me. You screwed up and you were punished for it. You're forgiven, but don't ever assume a choice again when it's not expressly given. Nod if you understand me."

She nodded passionately, her wide expressive eyes communicating everything she couldn't say. *I'm sorry. I hate to displease you. Please smile at me and tell me everything's okay.* With a small sigh, he traced fingers across her tearstained cheek, then leaned down to kiss her. She shuddered, closing her eyes. Such delicate lids, fluttering with emotion.

He cradled her face in his hands, feeling his own strange wave of sentimentality. He turned away, schooling his thoughts back to his purpose. Training. Slave development. "We won't let this derail the progress you've made. The party's starting soon and I want you at your best. You'll serve in whatever way is requested. Everyone there will be a trusted friend or client who can be depended on to follow the rules. You play your role...slave and plaything. And obviously," he added with emphasis, "you are not to come. You will exist tonight for others' pleasure, not your own. Nod if you understand me."

She nodded again, and he led her out to the kitchen to eat, and then to wash up and have the plug removed. He buckled his own house collar around her neck above her slim silver one—a signal she was club property to be shared—and led her out to the main area just as the other help was starting to arrive.

* * * * *

Mephisto enjoyed orchestrating sex parties. Maybe it wasn't a traditional career choice, but it was his career choice and he took , pride in doing it well. Often they were anything-goes type orgasm

80

blasters, but other times he enjoyed more structured events, with a clear delineation of who was bottom and who was top.

Tonight's party would be one such party. All the bottoms—seven females, including Molly, and three males—wore collars. All the tops—and there were significantly more—didn't need anything to broadcast their dominance. This collection of players simply oozed dominance from within.

Mephisto watched Molly, entertained by the way she was simultaneously trying to stare and appear submissive at the same time. There was certainly a lot of cock to look at. Mephisto had invited thirty male tops to attend, and only five had declined. It wasn't long before Molly was grasped from the corral of subs and slaves and put to work sucking off a well-hung gentleman. Other females were shared by their Masters, many of them strapped to dungeon equipment and tormented for the entertainment of the assembly.

Mephisto kept an eye on it all with the help of some dungeon monitors. Of course, everything that went on was consensual. His monitors had instructions to break in and question any s-type who seemed too spacey to use a safe word. There was a line as far as brutality, and his usual patrons knew not to cross it.

Soon the tops were doubling up on the bottoms, one of the prime reasons he maintained such an uneven ratio for his parties. The tops liked the power trip of ganging up on the bottoms, and the bottoms...well... He only had to look at Molly, filled with cock on either end, to know that she was turned on. One man was buried in her throat while another knelt behind her, drilling her asshole. Her butt was still red and undoubtedly sore from his hand and his belt, not to mention the other various beatings of the past few days. At least her whip marks were fully healed.

The other bottoming girls and guys found themselves similarly occupied. Two of the male bottoms were ordered to fuck while a group of tops surrounded them and watched, shouting ever-raunchier instructions. Another was being alternately beaten and fucked while strapped to a spanking bench. Mephisto loved the exuberance of male bottoms, but he also loved the vulnerability of the girls. Lila was sobbing in one corner, straddling a wooden horse and having her nipples tortured with a crop. A few of the other subs were hard at work sucking off and rimming their Masters.

Lorna had been annoyed not to be invited, but it always caused problems to mix dommes in with a bunch of male dominants on a testosterone binge. Somehow, one or two always decided the dommes secretly wished to submit, and only needed to be taken in hand by the right man. Funny to watch, but a distraction at best. At worst, a trip to the emergency room to have a stiletto heel removed from a rectum. No, the dommes got their own night.

Testosterone issues aside, Mephisto knew all these men, respected them all as responsible players in the scene. They were long time friends of the club to be invited to such a party, and most of them willingly shared their slaves if they were in a relationship. The majority of the straight ones took a turn with Molly, even if it was just a grope or a slap. Clayton rarely shared, especially at big parties like this, so the men were taking their shot while they could. She ended up taking a lengthy flogging shackled to a St. Andrew's Cross, followed by fucking in her pussy and ass. Well, he'd warned her about the assfucking, not that she seemed to mind it. He could see it in the way she breathed, her facial expressions. She was so hot, so horny. So unsatisfied.

All the orgy guests understood that she was on orgasm restriction. Some of them teased her on purpose, while others used it as an excuse to fuck her quickly and mechanically, treating her as a disembodied sex doll. Knowing Molly, that probably turned her on most of all.

Next, Molly endured a trip over the spanking bench at the behest of his friend Aaron, who had a strong penchant for rattan canes. Mephisto knew Aaron knew what he was doing, but Molly still suffered. Every so often, as Molly screamed and struggled in her bonds, Aaron would walk around the bench and tighten the screws on her nipple clamps. Devious. Mephisto watched the whole scene with his cock bucking in Lila's mouth. Molly's ass had to be killing her though. She crawled back to the corral at the end of Aaron's arm and settled back very gingerly on her heels. Her face was a mask of distress and discomfort. If only she realized that made her even more attractive to the tops, most of whom were sadists like Mephisto.

Low, sultry house music throbbed over the speakers, an aural bump and grind to accompany the players' movements. Again and again Molly was beckoned, clutched, subdued, clamped, impaled. She was double penetrated with cocks and dildos, made to suck cock after cock, sometimes more than one at the same time. No sooner was she released from a top than another cock would be pressed against her pussy or her ass. She was slapped, nudged, forced to the ground and pulled up again for more usage. She grew tearful but she never cried, never resisted. And in all this, all her dismay and confusion, Mephisto observed her unmistakable arousal. What must that feel like to be fucked over and over, to be, as a masochist slave, used repeatedly and cruelly and not permitted to come? For a normal woman, it would have been hell. For Molly, it was teasing beyond belief.

As the third hour passed, the party began to wind down. The bottoms were used up, the tops were fucked out. The other subs had had no prohibitions against orgasm. Most of them left on their Masters' arms glowing and satiated. His own orgasmic Lila had come several times, twice at his own hands. Only Molly still seethed with unassuaged need and longing. He only had to look at her to know she was dangerously worked up. He applied some clover clamps to take the edge off her sex high and cuffed her firmly to one of the crosses until he could see off the rest of the guests.

He took his time returning to her. Ten minutes at least, and she was still simmering on high boil in her bondage and clamps. He smiled at her and reached between her legs to find an ocean of wetness. Since all the men had worn condoms, it came from only one place—her own frustrated body. He slid fingers through her juices and tapped her clit, just once. She sucked in her breath and jerked as though he'd slapped her. Her eyes were wide and wet as he leaned closer. A cornered animal indeed.

"You're wound so tight, my lovely little slavegirl," he murmured. "Would you like me to touch you again?"

She gasped and shook her head, then nodded. He laughed. She was truthful at least, in her crisis. "I don't think I'd better. I'm going to release you now." He uncuffed her hands and for a moment she just held them stiffly at her side, as if she feared being in control of them again.

Ah, her gaze was so desperate. She was in so much erotic pain, clamps notwithstanding. His poor slave wanted to come so, so badly. He tapped her clit just a moment, a whisper of a touch. She sobbed...reached out for him...and then toward her mons.

He slapped her hand away firmly. "No."

To his disbelief, she tried again. Right to his face, right in front of him, she defied him. He trapped her arms in one hard grip and slapped her. "I said no." She tugged at her wrists, but he raised his hand again in warning. Jesus. She did have a breaking point, and she'd just reached it. He shook his head at her, frowning. "You were such a good girl at the party. But you're not being a very good girl now. Put your hands on your head."

She started to cry. She was falling apart. He had to get her to bed, because he sure as hell wasn't letting her come now. He released her ankles and unclamped her nipples and marched her to the bathroom. An ice cold shower cooled her down pretty quickly, but her miserable shame was still in full force. She couldn't beg, so she cried. When that didn't work, she cried harder. When he started oiling up the dildos on her harness with the teasing lube, she fell to her knees and sobbed into the floor like a feral thing.

"You were doing so well," he said as he harnessed her, just to exacerbate her misery.

He put her in the underbed cage, a claustrophobic, dark space for bad slaves who acted out. From there, she couldn't see him and he couldn't see her, which was by design. She was tightly contained, her needy pussy encased in its convex metal cup and the dildos filling those orifices aching to be satisfied. Her hands were cuffed at her waist so she couldn't even wipe her tears. He let her cry a long time, enjoying it at first. After an hour, his patience wore thin. She was the one who'd defied him. His word was law and she knew it, no matter how much she hated it, no matter how much she'd wanted to finger her pussy. It wasn't fucking allowed. It was what she'd signed up for, and what she had to live with. Finally, he banged on the side of the cage and ordered her to go to sleep.

The Sixth Day

He woke in the morning and stretched, feeling unusually rested. A rollicking orgy had a way of doing that. He looked at Molly's cage in the corner before he remembered that she was in the bad-girl cage beneath his bed.

He got up and showered and shaved, figuring he'd let her sweat it out in the cage a little longer, but when he returned to peer through the bars at her, her eyes were closed. She was so still.

Oh my God, I killed her. Could a slave die from an orgasm denial regimen? She wasn't dead though, just wiped out. Her eyes moved faintly behind her lids, and her face was still criss-crossed with dried tear tracks from the night before. Her chest rose and fell, her sweet lips open just slightly so her breath whistled in and out. Since the very first night, she hadn't talked again in her sleep. He didn't realize until now how he missed it, that secret side of her. He still wanted to know all her secrets, but the week was almost over and he'd learned nothing at all.

He rattled the bars in a sudden fit of irritation. Molly's eyes blinked open and she too seemed to forget at first where she was. When she figured it out, shame washed over her features.

"Are you better now?" he asked.

She nodded, and he helped her crawl out. He removed her harness and washed her, then took her to the kitchen for breakfast. Not surprisingly, she had little appetite. He persisted, coaxing her to eat syrupy pancakes from his fingers and lick the stickiness clean. She drank thirstily and he refilled a water glass just for her. At some point during this quiet and intimate breakfast, he decided to take her out for a while. She'd been cooped up in his club for nearly a week. It wasn't good slave ownership. Like a flower, she needed fresh air and sun.

Clothes. She would need clothes, and his certainly wouldn't fit her. Over the years he'd accumulated a fair amount of female clothes in his spare room, which he laundered and put away for emergencies such as this. He gave her a warning look and left her alone, unharnessed and unsupervised. Hell, if she masturbated now, he'd throw in the towel, but he knew she wouldn't. He found some jeans, a tee shirt and pale green sweater that looked to be around her size.

When he returned to the kitchen and held them out to her, her mouth dropped open in surprise. Her features broadcast worry and confusion.

"It's okay, we're going out," he said. "It's a beautiful day and you haven't gotten much exercise this week. Put these on. No panties and no bra. I don't want anything between me and you but these articles of clothing."

She dressed like she was doing something naughty and forbidden. He wondered how often, in her day-to-day life, she actually wore clothes. Not very often, he guessed. She kept plucking at the garments like she wasn't sure they were put on right, but she looked lovely. Fresh and conservative, like a co-ed on her way to class. The jeans accentuated her feminine form and the sweater was thick and cozy for the chilly early spring weather. Mephisto fingered her collar, removing the o-ring that betrayed the decorative band's true purpose.

"Vanilla enough, I guess," he said, smiling at her. She smiled back, even though she still looked a little bewildered. From deep slavery and a night in the bad-girl cage to a trip outside the walls. He decided to drive her to a park, and spent the whole way lecturing her about obedience, the importance of orgasm denial for discipline, and other slavey topics, basically just to turn her on. After that, he took some time to praise her for her sexual submissiveness the night before at the orgy. Through it all she listened attentively, her hands clasped in her lap. Her silence was like a third passenger in the car. So obvious, and yet unacknowledged by him. Better, she didn't even seem to feel the urge to speak. His quiet, mastered doll.

Only one more day.

Her Master would come for her tomorrow. Part of Mephisto would be relieved to see her go, but part of him had grown attached to her. He needed another damn week. The whole point had been for them to get to know one another, to gain some ease and understanding. But Mephisto was afraid the only understanding Molly gained was that she'd never willingly come near him again. He'd enjoyed exerting his authority over her, and she'd probably enjoyed parts of it too, but had they grown closer? It was hard to tell.

As they walked around the jogging path at the park, Mephisto watched the other groups of people. Couples, friends, families with children on bikes or scooters. All these people were involved in relationships, and so was he with Molly. Their relationship was just different. At one point he took her hand, not even thinking. *She's Clayton's. She's only yours on loan.*

They stopped at a snack bar, and he bought ice cream and popcorn. She looked so delighted that for a moment he almost lost his composure. It was just soft serve, for fuck's sake. He wanted to ask her if Clayton ever took her for ice cream, but he was afraid to hear that he didn't. He wanted to buy her a billion ice cream cones. Silly, when he wouldn't allow her even one orgasm. She licked the cone so sweetly, so happily, that he fed most of it to her, fixating on her lips and her tongue.

When the cone was gone, he ate the popcorn, occasionally feeding Molly and occasionally feeding the ducks waddling by. It didn't even occur to him at first that it might look strange, the way he fed her. Lots of couples fed one another, but that was usually flirtation. Impulsive sharing. For the entire week, Molly hadn't eaten anything that hadn't come from his hand. The idea of it hit him in his groin. He walked her a little way off the main path to a secluded bench and pulled her into his lap. He put his fingers to her lips and she licked off grease and popcorn salt with a grin that slayed him. When she finished he snaked his hand up her shirt, under her sweater, and pinched her nipples until she squirmed. Her breathing quickened and she shifted in his lap. He imagined her pussy moistening, her little clit hardening up once again, ever hopeful even though time after time arousal had ended in nothing but frustration this particular week. Physiology was an amazing thing.

And it worked both ways. She slid a hand around his neck—a forward, unrequested embrace—and he was too aroused to correct her. She rested her face against his cheek, making tiny, faint lust noises. His cock was straining, hard as rock. He squeezed her breast and groaned, wrapping his other hand in her hair. He pulled her head back and kissed her neck, her eyes. When she moaned into his mouth he broke away and looked around at the people in the park. "My own orgasm denial," he groused, exasperated. "For once, I feel your pain."

He took her hand and dragged her after him in search of privacy. Off a trail, in the back of the park, he found a remote wooded area. There, behind a curtain of thick brush and bushes, he had her kneel and serve him. It was a memory moment for him: the light breeze, the singing birds, and Molly's expression as she licked around his cock and sucked his balls. He curled his fingers into the bark of the tree beside him, feeling the scratchy solidness of it. The whole world seemed to shrink down to that one moment, that one sensation of Molly and nature and everything being in tune.

He bucked in her mouth, caressing her face, wanting to scream out all the things he felt. His wonder at her submission, the privilege, the specialness of it. *Tomorrow, she goes. Tomorrow, all gone.* He pushed that thought away, living in the moment, enjoying her skillful ministrations until his climax exploded and almost took him to his knees. Later today, he decided, he would let her come. He would give her an orgasm as special and memorable as this. He'd wanted to wait until the last day, but today would be better. He actually couldn't wait to see her fall apart with the power of all that pent-up lust.

With that thought, he zipped up and handed her the used condom. She leaned down and blithely buried it under a pile of dirt and leaves.

"Silly girl," he snorted. Silly, unfathomable, reckless girl. She was still reckless, he decided. It just manifested in different ways, like giving all her power over to another person. A carefully chosen person. Someday, that responsibility might be his.

Or perhaps not. Maybe someday she would choose not to be a slave anymore.

Mephisto took her hand and led her to another area of the park, a picturesque urban stream flanked by rocks, bushes and trees. Molly used to work for Seattle City Parks, monitoring stream life and pollution. She'd told him all about it one night while she was drunk. She'd been so impassioned about it. Did she even remember that now? She'd quit her job—or been fired—just a few weeks later. Had she ever been to this park? This stream? He searched her face for answers but she remained stubbornly expressionless.

A sudden breeze kicked up and rustled the trees, the tiny buds that bloomed in the new warmth of spring. Molly put her hands together in front of her lips like she was praying, and for a moment Mephisto thought she might speak, but she didn't.

She started to cry.

He could have asked her then, asked her all the things that Clayton wanted to know, that Mephisto desperately wanted to know too. *Are you happy? Are you sorry? Do you have regrets? What do you see in your future?*

What do those tears mean?

She turned to him and her expression said it all. *Just take me home. That's all I want, to escape this. Please don't ask me anything.*

So Mephisto took her home.

* * * * *

Back at the club, Mephisto watched Molly undress and fold her borrowed clothes into a perfectly aligned stack. He took the bundle and tossed it on the pile with the other things for the laundry service, only so he wouldn't be tempted to hide them away and fondle them like some sociopathic stalker after she was gone. Meh. He might still do that.

He reattached the o-ring to her collar and put her to work dusting and straightening up the dungeon. She moved around doing whatever task he set her to in perfect slave mode, as if her short brush with the outside world was some horror that proper service and submission could erase.

So be it. She was happy. He was glad to know it. She didn't yearn for all the things she'd lost when she went into slavehood, all the things she'd left behind. She yearned for her Master, Clayton, and if Clayton wasn't around, then him. So, to keep her happy, he continued to assign her the most menial tasks he could think up, while he worked at his desk and daydreamed about ways he could bring her to orgasm later. Some bondage, a little teasing to make her think she was in for more torture, and then—

He heard a shriek from the kitchen. He ran in to find her standing at the sink, fumbling with the faucet handle. She'd been ironing clothes for him, but the iron was lying on its side, the clothes knocked over in a jumble. He righted the hot iron and went over to her.

"What happened?"

Like some nightmare, some bad dream, she held out her forearm. The underside had an angry red mark down the middle. He grabbed it, staring down at the pristine velvet skin already puckering into blisters. "Fuck!"

He held it under the water. Clayton would fucking murder him for this. "Fuck!" he shouted again, so loud she flinched. He thought about her tears at the stream, her robotic slaveyness. "Did you do this on purpose?" He clenched her elbow as he yelled at her. "Did you?"

She shook her head, looking scared.

"Talk to me, damn it!"

"You put me on speech restriction!" She pulled her arm away from his rough grasp.

He gave her a quick, sharp slap across the cheek, for the sass and for the panic that even now had his heart pounding. Self-hurting slaves didn't fly with him. He'd been there, done that, read the book and written the review. He didn't fucking do that shit. He took a deep breath and grasped for calm.

"Forget the speech restriction," he snapped. "How the fuck did this happen?"

"It was an accident. I'm sorry!" He gazed into her eyes, searching for answers, and saw no guilt or premeditation, only pained shock. She didn't do it to herself. It was an accident. His breath came easier, but there was still his broken promise to explain to Clayton.

"I told your Master no permanent damage," he said. "No scars!"

Again she stared in miserable, tongue-tied helplessness. She must think him a maniac. *Breathe. Just breathe. Take care of her.* He unplugged the iron and hurried her back to the bathroom. He ran her arm under cold water a while longer, then dried her burn with the softest towel he could find. It stood out in stark relief against the pale skin of her forearm, half an inch wide, a couple inches long. "Jesus Christ," he yelled again as he wrapped the burn in a loose gauze bandage. "He's going to kill me."

"But it was my fault, Master," she said. "I'm not good at ironing. I should have told you."

He didn't want her to blame this on herself. He looked up, on the verge of snapping at her again, and she flinched. Jesus, he had to calm down. He was freaking her out and the pain of the burn had to be excruciating enough. He ran his hands through his hair and then led her back out to his work table. Should he take her to a hospital? A plastic surgeon?

"Sit here. Just sit here and don't move."

He went back to the bedroom and closed the door and dialed Clayton's number. Clayton picked up on the third ring.

"Mephisto. How are you today?" he asked.

I'm shitty. I maimed your slave. It's going to scar and there's nothing I can do about it. "There was— Molly had— There was an accident."

"What happened?" asked Clayton sharply. "Tell me."

"A burn," Mephisto forced out. "Nothing serious. She's okay. She got a burn. She was ironing."

"Ironing?" Clayton sounded incredulous. "She can't iron, my friend. You're lucky she didn't burn down your entire dungeon, and I'm sure she ruined your clothes!"

"Clayton—"

"How bad it is?" the other man asked.

"Not bad. A little blistery. Thin, a couple inches long. I'll take her to the hospital if you want."

"For a little burn like that? Answer me this, is she crying?"

"No."

"Just put some antibiotic cream on it and bandage her up, then. She's a slave, not a Ming vase."

"But I promised to return her free of scars. And I think this will leave a scar."

"You and I both know I was talking about impact scars. Not something like this. What's really the matter?"

94

Mephisto blinked, taken aback by his blunt question. He took a moment to think before he answered. "I wanted to return her to you in perfect shape. Exemplary condition, with lots of edifying and educating experiences. I wanted to improve her for you, and I'm not sure I've been doing that at all."

Clayton tsked softly. "You know what I've learned in my advancing age and experience? Owning a slave shouldn't be so much work. I really believe that. At some point you have to trust them to serve you. Not with trials and tests, and hoops to jump through, and some measurable result. Sometimes you have to just appreciate what's in their hearts. Tell me this. What kind of condition is Molly's heart in at the moment?"

Mephisto sighed. "Pretty good condition, I think."

"Is she still on orgasm restriction?"

"Yes."

"Perhaps it's time to release her from that. And release yourself a little too." Clayton paused. "What's in *your* heart, my friend?"

Molly. Molly is in my heart, goddamn you.

Mephisto hung up with Clayton a few minutes later, promising to give Molly an orgasm spectacular enough to distract her from the pain of her burn. That part would be easy. Saying goodbye tomorrow would be hard. Would she miss him? She had a scar to remember him by, if nothing else.

"Master," she said as soon as he came back to her. "It—it already feels better."

Lovely, lovely girl. She deserved to feel better. She was really such a lovely, obedient girl. "I need to see you in the bedroom," he said.

She followed, not questioning. Perhaps she expected him to beat her, or tease her some more, or put her back in the dreaded harness. None of it mattered to her; she would do as he asked and so all the decisions lay with him. It was such a shocking level of trust, and, as Clayton had reminded him, that came not from practice and trials, but from her heart. In the bedroom, he drew her close and ran his fingers through her soft, curly hair. He stroked her injured arm and kissed her wrist just above the loosely wrapped bandage. "Your Master misses you," he said. He looked at her as if he expected an answer, because he wanted to hear her voice.

"Oh. You talked to him?"

"Yes."

Yes, I talked to him. Yes, you and I are talking now. Yes, I want to feel you shake and cry out under me with all that passion in your heart. He ran his fingers over her breasts, across her flat belly and down to the apex of her thighs. He kissed her, tasting loyalty and courage and that note of sweetness that destroyed him as much as it turned him on. He stripped off his shirt and dropped his jeans to the floor. Molly started to her knees but he stopped her.

"No."

He nudged her toward the bed and bent her over it, studying the welts on her ass. Those lines and bruises told the narrative of her stay with him. He touched each one, remembering, and then kissed her from the base of her spine up to her nape. She shivered, parting her legs a little more as he nestled his hips between her thighs. He wanted to thrust into her as he was, naked and unsheathed. He wanted to feel that closeness, that connection to her, even though it wasn't a possibility. He pulled away with a curse, going for a condom. He rolled it on and took her hips in his hands, teasing her pussy with the head of his cock. She was so warm, so eternally wet.

"Molly..." He said her name, not *girl* or *you* or *slave*. He felt her body tense, grow rigid for a moment, but she was Molly to him, always, before everything else. She always would be. He sank deeper, pressing all the way in with attention to every sensation, every pinging of his nerves. Her hips moved slightly, raised and arched back toward him. He reached beneath her and parted her, sliding his fingers through her slickness and finding her swollen clit. He pressed it, teased it. He was deliberately slow, trying to stoke a long, hot burn rather than a quick explosion. She thought he was just edging her. He could tell it in her tension, her reservation, and yet she responded to him anyway. How selfless she was. What a good slave.

As if she read his thoughts, she turned her head and whispered in her steady, submissive way, "Master, I'm yours."

Good God, why had he restricted her speech the whole week? Her voice was such a potent aphrodisiac, just like her scent, her body, her deep blue eyes. His teeth closed on her neck and he bit her gently, provoking a delicious sigh and shudder. At the same time, he slid forward into her, seating himself fully, basking in the pressure of her pussy around his cock. She moaned and fell forward, gasping as her injured arm brushed across the bed.

He pulled out and lifted her, turning her over. "Hold onto me," he said. "Let me hold you."

He entered her again and she arched beneath him, wrapping her legs around his hips. She reached out for him and he leaned forward, amazed to feel her stroking him, pulling him closer. She twisted her fingers in his dreadlocks and snapped her hips against him, giving more of herself, offering herself for his pleasure. He stared down at her, wanting to hold this moment forever. He was wrong. He had taught her something. He'd taught her that she could withstand all his torments, that she could prevail and be a better slave for it. And she...she had taught him that she was so much more than a slave. Always more than a slave.

He made a sound, just a small sound, but her gaze flew to his and something passed between them. A spark. An understanding. He nodded to her, past words now. How to explain this? Any of this? It wasn't necessary. She understood what he wanted from her. She closed her eyes and launched herself at him, gripping his neck. She held tight, her pussy clenched around his cock, milking him, sending heat to his balls and down his thighs. They moved together in a lust-fueled dance, all caution to the wind. They were creating the blue kind of fire, the long-slow-burn fire he wanted for her. It was going to burn them both.

He pulled her closer, his delicate little balsawood airplane, thrusting and straining against him. He was the rubber band, twisting around and around her and holding her tight.

"Fly for me, Molly," he growled against her ear.

She scratched his back and gasped, and then they were coming together in a bursting frenzy. He exploded like a bomb, howling out her name. He could feel her orgasm go on and on, her body quaking under his, her little sobs the most erotic music in the world. They collapsed together, gasping in the aftermath. Two hearts beating wild, connecting on some new unforeseen level.

Again, Mephisto thought. *I have to have her again, and again.* He had to remember this. He had to consign this to memory—this slow, splendid burn like nothing he'd ever felt.

The Seventh Day

Mephisto dreamed of her all night, dreamed of fucking her and bringing her to orgasm. He dreamed of the look in her eyes when she understood he was going to let her come. He relived her shudders and the hot pleasure of burying his cock in her pussy and her ass, over and over, her body sliding against his, trapped under his, writhing in release.

Then he woke to a dream made real. He groped for a rubber and parted her legs from behind, pressing inside her, still half asleep. She moaned and arched back against him. For a while they fucked just like that, lazy and drifting, but with each thrust, more memories returned. More wicked, sex-drenched memories. His caresses intensified, and he fucked her harder, deeper. They were both waking up now, waking up on this...their last day.

He sat up and turned her around, lifted her into his lap, driving her down onto his cock. He manipulated her hips, wanting to be deeper, all the way inside. He kissed her hard, then pulled her head back with a fist in her hair and closed his teeth on her neck. They were fucking like animals, wild and uninhibited. Mephisto wondered if she and Clayton ever fucked like this. He felt quite certain they didn't. Clayton was too controlled for this kind of sex. This was Molly, the old reckless, fun-loving, hard-living Molly giving him everything, damn the consequences.

It turned into a kind of struggle, a wrestling match. Mephisto dumped her back on the bed with a grunt, pinning her down, yanking her legs up over his shoulders. He squeezed her breasts and almost slapped her—just for fun—but then instead pressed a hand against her windpipe. She gazed up at him with lustful adoration. *Yes, lovely girl, I could kill you if I wanted to—but you know I won't.* He released her with a bark of a laugh and leaned to kiss her. Their liplock ended in a bite—hers, not his. Little savage. He chuckled and grabbed her hands, pinning her arms over her head. He pressed his hips against her, forcing her legs wider with his knees, his ankles pinning her feet.

The tighter he held her, the more she squirmed beneath him, and the harder he fucked her. When he growled for her to come, she fought him and kicked her legs, hopelessly spread and conquered. Her cries rose to gasping, pleading utterances, and then he felt her whole body tense up. Her pussy contracted around his length, and his balls drew up in delicious erotic tension. While she flailed through her orgasm, he twisted her hair in his fingers and rode her to his own peak. She gasped as he pounded her, hurt her, but her orgasm rolled on, long past the time his left him feeling satisfied and empty.

Finally, she subsided, going limp. He pulled away to get rid of the condom, then slid back into the bed beside her, gathering her close to drink in her last few shudders, her shaky breaths. That was it. He wouldn't let her come again with him. It was time to turn her mind back to her Master. Her real Master. Mephisto held her close and pressed his cheek against her forehead.

"Today's the day."

He took great care to make his voice sound neutral. Not happy, or disappointed. Not enthusiastic or mournful, although he felt a little mournful. He leaned back to watch her face. He saw the anticipation and gladness he expected, but a little shadow of sadness too. Maybe he was just imagining it.

"Show me your arm," he said.

She held out her bandaged limb and he unwrapped it carefully. God, they'd fucked like monkeys for the last twelve hours. He hoped they hadn't aggravated her injury. He uncovered her burn, but fortunately it seemed to be healing. Still red, but no longer swollen, and no blisters.

"It looks better," he said.

"Yes, Master."

"It's possible I overreacted yesterday."

Molly laughed softly. "I'm so clumsy sometimes. My Master knows it. He'll just shake his head when he sees this."

"Yes. He didn't sound too surprised yesterday on the phone. He was actually shocked that you hadn't managed to get yourself into more trouble."

She lowered her eyes. "Did you tell him about...everything, Master?"

"Not yet, but I will. The good and the bad. He might as well know the things you were punished for, as well as the things you handled well."

But he wouldn't tell him everything. He wouldn't tell Clayton about those times he saw the real Molly, his old Molly. Somehow he wanted to keep that to himself. She gazed up at him with wide eyes, fidgeting slightly at his side.

"What?" He stroked her cheek. "What now?"

"Are you really going to give him the harness?" she asked in a small voice.

"Yes. But now you're asking too many questions. You can ask me one more thing about our time together. Anything. But only one more thing, so choose carefully."

He thought she must have an untold number of questions about their week together. He thought she'd take a while to narrow down to the one she wanted. But she asked quickly, and she asked directly. "Why did you take me out to the park yesterday? To that creek?"

Fuck. That was a hard question. He let out a long breath, brushing his lips against her temple. "I just really wanted to see you there. I had my own questions."

She made a slightly annoyed face. She couldn't ask what those questions were now, having used up her one chance, and he wouldn't have told her anyway. *I just wondered if you were happy. I want you to be happy. I think you are, but I can never be sure...because I can control everything but your truths.*

She looked over at the cage, and Mephisto was amused to detect a note of wistfulness in her expression.

"Will you miss the cage?" he asked with a smile.

"I... I think I will miss it a little, Master. It was a nice place to feel safe. To feel your control."

"You can spend some time in there after breakfast. I don't need you for anything." He traced over her breasts, teasing her nipples. She gave a little shiver and pressed closer to him.

"Master... Am I still... May I...?"

"Don't even think about it." He shook his head at her in mock reproach. "Greedy girl. Yes, our time is almost up and the rules are relaxing a little. But I think you've had plenty of orgasms for the moment. If anything, I need to get you more worked up for your reunion with your Master. It's the least I can do for him, after he was kind enough to share you with me."

He fed her breakfast, remembering that first day she'd knelt there in his kitchen, her eyes wide and nervous, her body drawn up tight. He hadn't known her body then, but he knew it now. Knew every mole, every freckle, every erotic hotspot. How long would he remember after she was gone?

But he had to get her ready for Clayton. He put some mild clamps on her nipples so he could leave them on for an effective amount of time, then harnessed her up tight with the stinging oiled-up shafts in her ass and pussy. She crawled into the cage with a woebegone look he'd certainly miss. An hour later he took off the clamps and, just for fun, loosened the harness just enough to slip a remote-controlled vibrator down inside it. He might as well play with her while he had her. An afternoon of edging would have her in tip top shape for her Master. It was the least he could do.

* * * * *

At dinner, Mephisto added another chair to the table. Molly stared at it from her knees. He waited for the gears to turn. She appeared traumatized, but he persisted.

"I know you know how to use a chair. Sit."

He unpacked takeout food, salads and sandwiches, as Molly sat wringing her hands in her lap. So she didn't want to act as his equal. What she didn't understand is that even sitting next to him at his table, even with her own plate, cup, and set of silverware, he was still in charge. The rest was Kabuki Theater. Even last night, when he'd held her like a lover and whispered in her ear, he was in charge. When she was having orgasm after orgasm, oblivious to everything else, including him, he was in charge of that too.

Maybe she did understand. Maybe she was upset because she understood his actions for what they were. A transitory process. The beginning of release. He heard a small sound, and looked over to find her crying. Still trying to eat. He stroked her hand to calm her.

"It's okay to cry. But I would like you to tell me the reason."

She looked up at him, blinking through tears. "I think it's mostly...that I'm going to miss you."

It was hard, really hard not to react to that emotionally. "I'll miss you too," he said as evenly as he could. "I enjoyed our time together."

"Me, too," she said, latching onto his neutral tone like a life raft. "I enjoyed serving you, Master."

"Are you happy?"

He asked it fast, while she was open and unguarded. He watched closely for her reaction, but she played dumb. "What do you mean? Happy to see my Master?"

"I mean," he said with a touch of impatience, "are you happy? Are you content in your life with him?"

She was back to twisting her hands in her lap. "Why are you asking me this?"

"Because he asked me to. And because I hope you would confide in me if you weren't happy."

"I am happy. Very happy!"

"He would love you either way, you know. He told me to tell you that too."

Molly gawked, trying to process those shocking words. Of course, in some way, she had to know they were true. But the color drained from her face as she stared at Mephisto. "Does he not... Does he not want...?"

Mephisto tsked. "Don't worry, kitten. It's your happiness he's worried about. As you know, he does what he wants in life, and his needs are well met by a very talented companion." He took one of her curls and pulled it in a soft tease. "He wants to be sure you're happy too, and he doesn't completely trust you to tell him the truth when you're in role. Not that a well-trained slave like you would lie. It is only," he said, brushing back her hair, "that slaves sometimes feel they must tell Master what he wants to hear."

He was trying to reassure her, to let her know it was okay, at this moment, to share her feelings, but she was in abandonment-alarm mode. "You're telling me the truth? He's not making plans to let me go, to release me? If you know—please—you have to tell me!"

Her panic was a tangible thing. It pained Mephisto to watch her go through it. Clayton was right. She really would fall apart if Clayton was ever forced to leave her behind. Mephisto disguised his concern in a sharp, chiding tone. "Release you? I never said anything about him wanting to release you. He's never indicated anything like that to me. In fact, I don't think there's any other owner of my acquaintance who cares so deeply about his slave. Just calm down, Molly."

Mephisto grimaced and took a sip of water, feeling suddenly, inexplicably irritable. *Molly, Molly...you're stronger than this. Aren't you?*

"You know, I did this to you," he said. "I made you who you are."

"That's not true. I was always meant to be this way. You're not God. You didn't make me any way—"

"Okay." Mephisto put his hand over hers. "Breathe, Molly. And you're right. I didn't make you into a slave, but I had a lot to do with introducing you to Clayton. I set you on this path. To be honest, I was surprised where it ended up."

"Surprised how?"

He sucked in air and let it out. "Surprised at how much you gave up for him." Their gazes locked. For a moment, just a moment, she was there. Really there. "Are you happy, Molly?"

She swallowed, wiping away the last of her tears. "Yes." Her voice was calm, reassuring. "Yes, Mephisto, I'm happy."

He was quiet a moment. He believed her, thank god. "Slavery fits you like a glove, kitten. So it doesn't surprise me. But look in my eyes and promise me that if you ever need help, you'll come to me. If you're ever unhappy. If the fit starts to slip."

"I promise," she said.

"Good enough." It had to be good enough. If this week had taught him anything, it was that Molly was strong, and that she was doing what she wanted. She was happy. Thank god.

They finished eating and straightened up the kitchen. Mephisto took off her harness and had Molly clean it and pack it away in a gift bag. It would be a gift for Clayton, not Molly, of course. Would Clayton use it? Would Molly miss it if he didn't? Mephisto got her tidied up and leashed, and walked her out to await her Master's arrival.

As his staff arrived for the evening and Club Mephisto prepared to open, Mephisto tugged at Molly's leash under his desk. He unzipped and sheathed himself, then put his head down in his hands and pressed the heels of his palms against his eyes. As dungeon monitors checked equipment and wait staff prepped the bar, he breathed in and out slowly, feeling nothing but her warm mouth and busy tongue, thinking of nothing but Molly. All those little looks. Those frustrated cries. Her longing, her anger, her submission. Her secrets. Her sweetness.

As his mind drifted, his cock was bucking, pulsing, reaching for orgasm under her talented attention. He thought of her on the bank of the creek, that look of loss, and yet determination. Everyone made choices in life. He thought of her delight as he fed her the ice cream. Vanilla ice cream, ironically. The laughter in her eyes and the delicate licks of her tongue...

She was happy.

He put a hand on either side of her head and emptied himself in her mouth, arching forward, his eyes shut, his mouth open in pleasure. He felt her tears warm against his palms. Beautiful emotional tears. If she wasn't happy, none of this would be a turn on. None of this would be okay.

She cried a little more before she settled and curled up under the desk at his feet. Her Master arrived a couple hours after the club opened, and Mephisto tugged her leash to alert her. Molly crawled out and sat up, watching Clayton approach, her shoulders straight and trembling as they'd been when he left. Her thighs slightly parted, her hands open in her lap. A slave presenting for her Master, waiting for his attention. His embrace.

The reunion was sweet. Formal and yet abandoned. Clayton greeted her, then pulled her up and hugged her, and she sank into his arms like a lost child finally home again.

When Clayton kissed her cheeks, tasting her tears, Mephisto had to look away.

A Week Later

Mephisto asked Clayton to meet him at the park rather than the restaurant Clayton suggested. He wasn't sure why. Maybe because he missed Molly.

Clayton wasn't a park type of guy, but Mephisto found him waiting at the bench by the snack bar anyway, just as agreed. The older man was enjoying a soft serve vanilla cone, his suit jacket folded neatly to the side over the arm of the bench. He looked like any typical real estate magnate getting some fresh air, one tailored pant leg crossed fastidiously over the other. He was authority and wealth personified, even on a rusting park bench. Damn him. Mephisto felt shabby in comparison, his dreads carelessly tied back.

Mephisto nodded at the half-eaten cone in Clayton's hand. "Molly loves that kind of ice cream."

"Does she?" His friend's voice communicated disinterest. Mephisto hated him for a moment. Clayton gestured to the bench and Mephisto seated himself beside him.

So how's Molly? Did she settle back in? These were the questions Clayton expected him to ask, perhaps, but Mephisto sat instead in silence. He felt churlish, antagonistic. Clayton finished his cone while Mephisto watched the joggers and walkers, the moms with baby strollers circling the park.

"I appreciate you watching Molly for me last week," Clayton finally drawled. "Although it's nice to have her home. She likes her routines. And her orgasms, you mean, mean man."

Mephisto shrugged, his hackles subsiding. "You are far too lenient with her, orgasm-wise."

Clayton gave an undignified snort and then they were both laughing. "I think she understands the purpose behind orgasm denial," Clayton said. "But she hates it just the same."

"Oh, yes, she understood." Mephisto sobered. "How's her burn?"

"Fine. Barely visible at this point. I hope you didn't tear yourself up too badly over it."

"If she was my slave, I wouldn't have. But she was on loan, and I felt like world's shittiest slave minder."

"I don't let her anywhere near the iron. Ever. I should have told you. I also keep her away from stovetops. Grills. Caustic chemicals, batteries. Ladders. Ice picks. Really anything that an overly exuberant slave might manage to maim herself with accidentally." He paused, toying with the cuff of his pants. "She is so pure of heart though."

"Like a child," Mephisto agreed. "Or a pet."

"An accident-prone pet."

They talked for a while about Molly's stay, about Mephisto's chastity training, about Molly's time at the orgy, about her slave highs and lows. Mephisto left out some things, but was brutally honest about others, like the fact that he'd punished Molly harshly

109

for something she hadn't even done. Clayton listened, inserting funny comments and observations. It reminded Mephisto that as much as he thought he knew Molly, Clayton knew her better. Clayton had a line on Molly that eclipsed anything Mephisto had managed to work out in a week. But that's why Clayton was her Master, and Mephisto only a temporary wrangler. That's why Clayton wasn't jealous of Mephisto. He had no need to be.

By the time Mephisto got to the end of his tales, both men were relaxed and chuckling about the one thing they both adored in common—Clay's very sweet and dedicated slavegirl. Clayton took a deep breath.

"Well, as I said, should anything ever happen to me..."

"Here we go again."

Clayton rubbed his forehead, his eyes on some point in the distance. "You know, I've had a good life. A superb life. A better life than any heartless old bastard like me deserved to have. I've had the best wine, the best women, the best homes, the best possessions, the best cars and travel, and of course, Molly to kneel at my feet these last few years. When I go, I'll go happy, and I have no children to worry about. Only Molly." He looked at Mephisto. "Thanks to you, I have the luxury of knowing she'll be taken care of. That means a lot to me."

"I understand that, but I hardly think you're at death's door. Why are you obsessing about this stuff? The big 5-0 on the horizon?"

"Maybe." Clayton uncrossed his legs and kicked at a pebble on the ground. "I could die in a car accident tomorrow, you know."

"Yeah, so could I."

"Well, don't. I'm counting on you if my chances run out."

Mephisto studied his friend. Something in his expression was off. "What's the matter, Clay? Really, what's this all about?"

The toe of his expensive Italian shoe sent the pebble skittering across the path. "Nothing's the matter." He looked up at Mephisto with something much closer to his usual smile. "I'm a businessman. I'm obsessed with being prepared. I did finally tell her about you, that you would look after her if something happened to me. But I kept it light."

"She still cried though, didn't she?"

"Like a faucet. Soaked my shirt. I think I set her worrying about that chastity belt. She knows that's what awaits her if she ever falls into your hands again."

That brought a smile from Mephisto, a strained chuckle. "She hated that thing. You should have heard the sounds she made every time I brought it out."

"I hung it on the back of the bedroom door. I look at it every so often very pensively just to freak her out."

Mephisto laughed out loud. "You're a sadist."

"You're more of a sadist. Molly told me enough of your adventures to know that." Both men laughed, finding peace in humor—at Molly's expense of course.

As Mephisto's laughter wound down, he sighed in mock disgruntlement. "I tried, Clay. I wanted to improve her for you, make her an even better slave than she already is. But I don't think I changed her at all. There aren't many ways to improve a girl like her."

"You made her more grateful for me, anyway. I appreciate that."

Mephisto grinned in response, but he felt miserable inside. "I was probably too hard on her. I can't help the way I am. I'll understand if you'd rather line up someone else to look after her. You know, in your Doomsday papers."

"Tell me something," Clayton said abruptly. "Do you love my wife?"

Mephisto's eyes went wide. "Well... I... You know—"

"You don't have to admit it to me, Jay. But I suspect you do. It would please me if you did. I think you could make her love you quite easily. In fact, I would give her to you now if I wasn't so selfish."

"You wouldn't," Mephisto blurted. "You can't. You... shouldn't."

"I should. But I won't."

"Are you thinking of..." Mephisto's words came out strained. He had to clear his throat and try again. "Are you thinking of releasing her?" Mephisto thought many times how difficult a job it must be, micromanaging a slave 24/7. Maybe Clayton was getting fed up with it. With her. "I told Molly you wouldn't ever release her," Mephisto said. "If you're thinking about letting her go—"

"Would you be there to gather up the pieces?"

"Yes, but you shouldn't. You shouldn't let her go, man. There's no one on earth like her, no one as loving and dedicated and fascinating and—"

Clayton chuckled softly over his words. "You do love her."

Mephisto sucked in a breath and let it out. "She belongs with you." *She always belonged with you. I always knew it, as much as it pained me.* "She needs you, Clay."

Clayton waved a hand. "I have no intention of releasing Molly. Ever. But if I die tomorrow, tell her you love her. She should know she's loved, even if she doesn't love herself enough." He scowled. "She doesn't, you know."

"Yeah, I know."

"I'll have to keep working on that with her. I tell her I love her but..." He shrugged. "She doesn't believe. She believes I love her

112

for what she does for me, not who she is. I don't know. I don't know what to do."

Mephisto was quiet a long moment. "You should buy her more ice cream," he finally said. "She really likes it. But you have to let Molly be Molly, you know? Appreciate what's in her heart."

Clayton gave a rueful nod for a point taken. If he was angry to have his words thrown back at him, he didn't show it.

"You are a very fascinating man, too, Mephisto," he said, "and I'll always be in your debt. Now, after this past week, you see why." Clay looked at him very directly. "But do you think she's happy? I know *she* thinks she is, but what do you think, having watched her this past week?"

Mephisto regarded his friend. "I know she's happy. I'm one hundred percent sure of it. I'm not so sure you're happy, which is kind of worrisome." He thought a moment. "Maybe Molly would benefit from a little more mental stimulation. You know, besides serving you. Maybe you both would. It might help you to see how strong she actually is. It might help you worry less."

"Molly, strong?" Clayton shook his head. "It's such a tightrope walk. She doesn't want any power."

"She doesn't need power to try something new. To take a college course online. To take up a new hobby." It was really none of Mephisto's business. He shrugged and looked away. "I don't know. It's just an idea. She's such an awesome little woman. If she was mine—" He clamped his mouth shut.

"If she was yours, then what?"

"Nothing."

"No, tell me. You won't offend me."

Mephisto sighed. "If she was mine, I would make her be Molly part of the time, whether she wanted to be or not. But that's just my style. I'm not criticizing you. I know your dynamic with her really works. So ignore me."

Again, Clayton chuckled. "I would never ignore you. I'm always open to new ideas. Although, you know what they say about an old dog and new tricks."

"You're not that old, damn it."

Again, Mephisto saw that look, that shadow cross Clayton's face. There was something he wasn't telling him. As quickly as he saw it, the look was gone.

"Make her be Molly," Clay said, repeating Mephisto's words. "But who is Molly? I still don't know. Maybe I never will." He stood with a sigh, brushing off his pants. "We'll be back at the club soon, me and my slave." He picked up his jacket and smoothed the wrinkles out, laying it over his arm. "Next week perhaps. I'll put her into chastity a few days before," he added with a wink.

With that he was off, back in business mode, with a wave over his shoulder. Mephisto watched him go, thinking about Molly and Clayton and secrets, and about his own promises to protect her. He wondered if Clay would start buying her more ice cream. Probably not.

Mephisto missed her so much already.

He headed back to the club in a strangely mellow mood, turning his mind to his own important duties. She wasn't his to miss. She wasn't *his*. He had to get over it.

When Molly needed him, if she ever needed him, he'd be around.

To be continued...

An excerpt from the romance novel
Burn for You
The conclusion to the Club Mephisto stories, now available.

"Master Mephisto?"

Mephisto turned at the sharp voice of his dungeon assistant, Glenn. "What is it?"

"A woman by the door. I think she's altered."

"If she's altered, she can't come in. You know the rules."

"I think it's Molly."

Mephisto spun toward the door. Glenn was right. It was Molly, but she barely looked like herself. Dirty, disheveled, her face and eyes swollen, probably from substance abuse. She yanked at her collar, screaming something he couldn't hear from across the room. Her eyes found his and she came storming his way, shrugging off the doorman trying to restrain her. She barreled right through a whip scene, evading injury by dumb luck.

"What the fuck is wrong with you?" Mephisto grabbed her arm and steered her to the side of the play space. "That singletail could have taken your eye out."

"Get it off me," she screamed, yanking at her neck, at the slim collar still gleaming there. "Take it off me, goddamn it. I know you know how."

The dungeon monitors were drifting closer in case Mephisto needed help, and patrons were starting to watch. Molly pulled at her collar like a full-blown maniac. She was on something, rabid, out of her mind. He dragged her back past the bar into his private rooms. He flipped on the light in the kitchen and looked down at the girl in his grasp. Her eyes were dilated, her skin pallid. She'd lost fifteen pounds at least since he saw her last. Six weeks ago?

"What are you on?" It came out a growl. Mephisto didn't allow drugs in his club and he didn't allow them in his life. "What the fuck have you been doing to yourself?"

She ignored him, pulling so hard on the collar he worried she'd injure her neck. She let out an ear rending scream. "Take it off! Get it off me!"

"Okay, I'll take it off. When you calm down, I'll take it off. Let go of it."

He took her hands, restraining her with some effort. There were garish bruises around her neck. Who knew how long she'd been trying to get it off? But pulling it right through her neck wasn't the way to do it. Her small hands struggled in his.

"Let go of me," she moaned. "Let go!"

"I'll let go when you stop fighting me. Don't touch it. I need a special tool to get it off but I won't go get it until you calm down."

She sucked in air. Some shred of awareness flickered in her eyes. Her gaze darted around his kitchen and she licked dry lips. He'd lay odds she was on some hallucinogen, not unknown for the old Molly. "Sit down," he said slowly and clearly. "Sit down and I'll take your collar off."

He led her to a chair at the table and she sank down. She shook all over, so hard he could almost hear it. She was in her usual pre-Clayton gear. Short skirt, nearly non-existent top. It was thirty degrees outside. He got a blanket from the bedroom and draped it around her. She reached again for the metal band around her neck, arrested by his disapproving sound. Glenn peeked in the door.

"Everything okay?"

"She'll be fine. Watch her a minute."

Mephisto hurried to the club's storage room, rooted through hardware and drawers of tools until he found the micro-screwdriver he needed. Molly wouldn't be the first slave he'd sprung from a "permanent" collar, nor would she be the last. He returned to the kitchen to find Molly glaring at Glenn with a murderous look.

"She's not quite herself, is she?" Glenn asked. "You want me to call anyone?"

"The loony bin?" Mephisto suggested. "Not for her. For me. No. She'll be fine, but I might not be back out there tonight."

"We'll hold down the fort."

Glenn left and Mephisto approached the sickly, shivering girl at his table. She seemed to be coming down already, her energy flagging. God knew how she'd gotten here in her condition. He could picture her wandering the streets of downtown Seattle, clawing at her collar and screaming like a psycho. What might have happened if she hadn't found her way to his place?

"Let me see." He reached for the shining eternity collar, pushing her knotted, lank hair to the side. Her hair used to be her crowning glory, thick and glossy and beautiful, but now it was dull, unwashed. She was trying to sit still but random shudders seized her small frame. "What are you on?" Mephisto asked again, now that she seemed slightly more lucid. "Are you going to go into heart failure on me? What did you take?"

"I don't know. I got it from someone."

"Who?"

She shrugged. "I don't know."

117

"Okay." He sighed, grasping for patience. "Where were you?"

"Somewhere. I don't remember."

"At home? At a restaurant? At a club?"

"A club. Somewhere."

Mephisto scrubbed a hand over his face. He had to get her collar off before she started yanking at it again. He traced around the smooth edges until he found the tiny depression he was looking for. "Be very still," he said. And then, "Are you sure?"

"Take it off." Her voice was firm. "I'm not his slave anymore."

Fair enough. He lined up the tiny screwdriver with the delicate, almost invisible release. She wasn't the only one shaking. His hands suddenly felt too big, too clumsy for this moment. He poked the sharp tool into the clasp until he managed to wiggle it loose. The collar opened and he eased it from her chafed neck.

She turned to him, breathing hard, her chest rising and falling. "Give it to me."

"No." Not a chance. She'd calmed somewhat, but she was still out of her mind.

"Give it to me!"

"The screaming won't work. You're not getting it until you're down. Here are your choices. Go to the hospital. Go to jail. Spend the night here."

She stood and moved toward the door. "I'm leaving. I'm going home."

He stepped in front of her with a grim look. "I'll repeat your choices one more time. Hospital. Jail. Here."

"You can't keep me here! You don't control me."

"It appears no one controls you. Even you."

"You can't make me stay here against my will. That's kidnapping."

"Okay. Jail then. Hospital will cost too much." Mephisto got out his phone.

"Give me that collar!" She launched herself at him but he held the collar over his head, subduing her with one tight arm around her waist. She flailed, spitting at him. "You're an asshole!"

"Yes, and an abuser. I remember."

"And a criminal!"

"Says the girl who's high on some illegal substance." He pulled her over to the sink and made her drink an entire glass of water, even though most of it ended up on his clothes, and then took her to the bathroom. "Sit down and piss," he said. "And if you dare go anywhere but in the bowl I'll fucking destroy your ass."

She scowled and used the toilet, then stood and defiantly kicked off her thong panties and wisp of a skirt. "Are you going to rape me now?"

"There is nothing on earth I'd find less appealing at the moment. Put your skirt back on."

"Fuck you."

With a sigh, Mephisto picked up her skirt and panties and carried them, along with the resisting woman, into his room. He flung her discarded clothes into a cage in the corner. Then he looked at Molly. "In you go."

"Fuck you!"

"One more time, because I know you're high and stupid right now. Hospital. Jail. Here. Pick your fucking choice."

She kicked him hard in the shin, which fucking hurt, then drew her knee back to aim for his balls. Before she could complete such an ill-advised attack, he forced her into the rectangular cage, shutting the door and locking it while she pounded on the bars. "You're going to be in so much fucking trouble when I call the police," she screeched. "This is kidnapping!"

"This is tough love. I'll let you out when whatever is in your system has worn off."

"I hate you. I hate you!" Bang, bang, bang on the bars. He sat on the edge of the bed and watched to be sure she wouldn't hurt herself. She banged for a minute, two minutes, but then she went still and lay back, and the sobbing started. Wails and sobs and threats of what would happen to him. "I have money, you asshole!" she shrieked. "I'm fucking rich. I'll ruin you!"

Mephisto wondered how much of Clayton's fortune Molly had managed to lose or burn through in the last month and a half. Not too much, he hoped. He shouldn't have left her alone, even though she sent him away. He realized that now.

"I hate you. I hate you. *I hate you.*" Screams turned to whines and whines turned to whimpers and then she was all raged out and there was only her vicious glare. He studied the slim metal circlet between his fingers, remembering better times. She followed him with her eyes as he stood and crossed the room to lay her collar on top of his chest of drawers. Such a beautiful, delicate work of art. He remembered when Clayton had first showed it to him. He'd had it specially made for her.

"It would have killed him to see you this way," Mephisto said. Not to her, because she was in no state to listen. He just said it because it was the dismal truth.

Burn For You is available now at Amazon.com, BarnesandNoble.com, All Romance Ebooks.com, and Smashwords.com.

About the Author

Annabel Joseph is a multi-published BDSM romance author. She writes mainly contemporary romance, although she has been known to dabble in the medieval and Regency eras. She is known for writing emotionally intense BDSM storylines, and strives to create characters that seem real—even flawed—so readers are better able to relate to them.

You can learn more about Annabel and her books at www.annabeljoseph.com. You can also like her Facebook page (www.facebook.com/annabeljosephnovels) or follow her on Twitter (@annabeljoseph).

Annabel Joseph loves to hear from her readers at annabeljosephnovels@gmail.com.

Made in the USA
Lexington, KY
19 September 2012